1

Russell woke a

erupted from the back of the van, his arm and head claiming the space between me and Penny, and thrashed wildly at the radio. 'Get it off! Get it off', he shouted, his arm flailing at the dashboard and hitting every button except the one he needed. Startled, Penny screamed. She lost control of the van which mounted the kerb.

Instinctively I reached out and turned off the radio. At that moment a lay-by appeared on our left and Penny brought the van to a halt. For a moment there was silence while the three of us got our breath back. Then Penny turned and stared at Russ.

'What,' she demanded, 'is wrong with you?'

'We can't have the radio on.'

'You could have killed us!'

'Yeah yeah, sorry about that. I was back there and I was half awake and it suddenly hit me that the radio was on.'

He thought for a moment.

'I might have panicked.'

Penny stared at him. 'You panicked because we were listening to the news?'

'I thought they might start playing music.'

None of this made any sense to Penny. I thought I knew what was behind it, though, so I shrank back into my seat and tried to keep out of it.

'I thought they might start playing music too,' she replied in her careful school teacher voice. 'That's why I put the radio on. So I could listen to it.'

'No, no music. I'm going cold turkey.'

'What?'

'I'm having a month without music. I'm not going to hear a single note.'

Penny considered this.

'Is that in case they play that shit song of yours?' she asked.

There was no good response to that. If Russ let it pass then that would be a tacit admission that we all knew which song she was talking about. If he asked which song she was referring to, he would be basically requesting abuse.

He let it pass. 'No music at all,' he told her.

Penny considered the implications of this.

'You mean... I'm stuck in this van... for a month... with you two... and no radio?'

'Yes.'

'No way!'

Russ nodded firmly. 'It's that or we go back now.'

She shook her head in disbelief.

'That's not possible,' she said. 'There's no possible way that you can go a month without hearing music.'

THE BRANDY OF THE DAMNED

The Brandy Of The Damned

By JMR Higgs

the big hand

Published by The Big Hand

First print edition 2012

www.bighandbooks.com
www.jmrhiggs.com

ISBN 978-0-9564163-5-3

CONTENTS

start here

PART ONE: WILL

Day 1 (Brighton) - Day 10 (Hill O' Many Stanes)

'Just because it's not possible is no reason to not do it.'

'What if you walk into a pub or a shop, and they have music playing?'

'Then I'll walk out again.'

During this conversation I attempted to hide by keeping still. It didn't work. Penny turned to me, seemingly unwilling to continue talking to Russ.

'You talk sense to him, Will.'

'I'll do no such thing', I informed her. 'I tried that once and no good came of it.'

She took a deep breath and, without saying anything else, undid her seat belt and left the van. There was a moment's silence after the echo of the slammed door died down before Russell leaned forward, trying to find her in the wing mirror.

He whispered to me. 'I can't see her. Can you see her?'

From where I was sitting I could see her leaning against the rear of the van, wrapping her arms deep inside her large baggy cardigan. Her head was down and a mass of curly hair covered her expression, but from the way she jabbed her running shoe into the dirt I saw that she was not particularly happy.

'Just about,' I whispered back.

'What's she doing?'

'Not much.'

'How does she look?'

I glanced back at the mirror. 'I've seen her happier.' I tried to shift my weight further into the back of the seat, to prevent her seeing me spying if she turned toward the mirror.

'Let's drive off and leave her.'

'No!'

'Yeah yeah, let's just go!'

'No, Russ', I said as firmly as I could.

'We might not get a chance again. And we can't put up with her for a month.'

'Russ, driving off and leaving someone by the side of the road is, on a karmic level, not a good thing to do.'

'You're thinking it through, stop that. It's not the time to think this through. If we just do it, if we drive off now and leave her, then I guarantee that by the end of the day we'll have convinced ourselves that what we did was not only right, but necessary, and even a little bit heroic and selfless on our part.'

I didn't feel that this was a matter that could be settled on the level of debate, so I gave him a stern look instead.

'If we leave her by the road then the three of us will all be happier,' he promised. 'Eventually.'

I shifted my stern face into a disapproving look.

'What's she doing here anyway? Why did she come? Why did you invite her along?'

'I didn't! I --'

At this point Penny opened the driver's door and I stopped in mid-sentence. She got back behind the wheel, politely ignoring the startled looks on our guilty little faces.

'Well then,' she said, 'no music for a month. This will be interesting.' Then she started the engine and pulled out back onto the road.

2

The following morning I woke early, thanks to the heavy, persistent rain beating on the roof of the van. I lay still, warm and unmoving in my sleeping bag, listening to the constant clatter on the tin womb surrounding me. It was comforting and threatening at the same time. This was a new feeling. I tried to name it, but couldn't. This was a promising start to our journey. When you're approaching middle age, any new feeling is a rare and valuable thing.

I laid still for an unknown length of time, listening. It had been nearly twenty years since I had last slept in that van. We had been a band then, the three of us, a three piece guitar band. I was the drummer, Penny played bass and Russell played guitar and sang. We had spent many months on the road, travelling, gigging and travelling again, making endless trips up and down the M1.

This was a long time ago, of course. I never thought I would find myself in these circumstances again. But sleeping in the back of van is like riding a bike, it turns out. It's a skill that never leaves you. It just leaves you with a few more aches and pains than you remember.

Occasionally I heard Russ shift slightly in the sleeping bag next to me. He was probably awake and listening like I was, but I had no reason to move my head and find out for sure. It felt then that we had already left normal life behind us, even though our journey was less than one day old. It felt like I was where I should be, which was odd because I had no idea what I was doing there.

The rear door of the van opened and the noise from the downpour rose to a roar. I looked up, and saw Penny's face peering out from under the hood of her winter coat. She studied the pair of us with a look that could almost have been affectionate. 'I've got three teas, and three bacon sandwiches,' she said.

Penny has a knack for minor miracles. There we were, in the early hours of a Tuesday morning in September, at a windswept bay in Kent in a constant downpour, and she had somehow found an open café. The rear door is hinged at the top so the three of us sat on the tail of the van, wordlessly chewing the warm bacon and staring out at the slate-grey sea, while the door above us kept us dry.

The rain was astonishing. Grape-sized splats of water fell with such force that the sea seemed to boil. It was twenty-first century rain, the type of rain we never had in the twentieth century but which has suddenly become commonplace. It felt like a flash-flood in waiting. This did not bode well for our journey around the coast, but there is definitely a certain something about such weather at the British seaside.

There had been an uncomfortable atmosphere in the van after the radio incident the day before. We had passed through Folkestone and Dover in silence. I had said nothing as we drove past signposts for all the places we had intended to stop, such as the Dungeness lighthouse or the White Cliffs themselves.

Eventually Penny turned off the Margate road and headed out to the north of Sandwich Bay. The van had come to a halt in an obscure little spot behind a golf course, looking out to sea. The handbrake clicked as she wrenched it up. Then she switched off the engine and turned to me.

'I know the plan was to spend the first night in Margate. But I've been to Margate, I've even busked there, and while I'm quite prepared to drive through it I will not spend the night there. Is that okay?'

It seemed reasonable. I nodded and she gathered her tent out of the back of the van. She erected this in the falling dusk, a discreet distance from the van. Then she climbed in and went to sleep without a word.

But that was yesterday. There was no reason why today had to be awkward. The magic of the bacon sandwich had given me a sense of optimism that even the weather couldn't erase. I gathered my confidence and asked the big, unanswered question. 'What are we doing this for, again?'

Russ turned and stared at me. 'What?'

'This whole trip. Driving around the coast of Britain.'

'Without listening to music,' added Penny.

'Not the music thing,' I clarified. 'That's some new weirdness.'

'Unfinished business,' said Russ.

Penny shrugged. 'Everything is unfinished business.'

'But all those years ago,' I said, 'when we first said we'd get in the van and follow the coast road – what was the reason?'

'Since when did we deal in reason?' asked Penny.

'There was a sort of reason.' said Russ. 'Maybe the word 'reason' is too strong. There was an idea.'

'A pretty bad idea,' said Penny.

'Yes, it was a pretty bad idea. But don't knock bad ideas. A lot of my best ideas are bad ideas. I can't really remember, though, it was so long ago. It was when we were writing *The Colour of the Sea*, wasn't it?'

Both Penny and I winced inwardly when we heard that title. Russ was referring to what would have been our third album, had we had stayed together and finished it instead of imploding under a weight of bad blood and unspoken resentment. *The Colour of the Sea* was Russ' preferred album title. It was a shit title which didn't mean anything, but that didn't bother me too greatly. We had used many shit titles by that point, and

I reasoned that one more wouldn't do any harm. Penny took a firmer line than I did, however, and fought it tooth and nail. There was a lot of fighting around that time, I remember. Penny and Russ had been a couple for most of the life of the band. They had been high-school sweethearts. The period between them stopping being a couple and the end of the band was not fun.

'It was around then,' Russ continued. 'Actually now I think about it, it wasn't an idea. It was a quest.'

'Was it?'

'It was.'

'It's not a very good quest though, is it?'

'No. It's not a very good quest at all. That's very true. But all the good quests have been done. Can you think of a good quest that hasn't been done?'

Penny thought.

'Going to Mars?'

'Apart from Mars. All the good quests have been done, apart from Mars. Only the second division of quests remain and most of them are pointless, like driving around the coast of Britain. But what can you do? We must make the best of what we have.'

'The thing is Pen,' continued Russ, 'Once you have a quest you pretty much have to go through with it, regardless of how stupid it is. Being a person who completed a stupid quest is nothing to be ashamed of. Being someone who embarked on a quest but gave up, on the other hand, is to be damned for life. It's harsh, but that's the way it is. And I know that nearly twenty years have passed but, if the van can take it, I will drive around the coast of this island, and then I'll look at myself in a mirror and see a man who completes whatever stupid quest falls to him.'

'And you'll end up back where you started.' said Penny.

'Probably,' Russell said. 'But the point of this quest is to question the unquestioned, to challenge the unchallenged presumptions that we build our lives on. Who knows how much of what we take for granted is fiction, passed on from generation to generation because people have better things to do than just ask really stupid questions? Actually, it's not aged very well, this idea, has it? Now I come to think about it again. Never mind. But our national identity is based on the idea that we are an island, and people have maps that seem to verify this, and we're happy to invest those maps with authority. How do we know that they're not lying to us? Have you ever met any mapmakers? No, we need to get on this road, and drive along the coast, and see where it goes.'

I was fairly sure that he was making this up as he went along.

'And if it turns out that it leads to where we started,' he continued, 'then that's a result in itself. We'll have gone nowhere, the long way round. But we'll know, we'll have certainty, that this is an island, and we are islanders, and that our journey was therefore utterly pointless.'

'It's a bit easier to get excited about quests like this when you're younger.' He paused to slurp his tea. 'But unfinished business is unfinished business.'

'Well okay,' said Penny. 'That was when you were young and creative. And had hair. But why now? Why are we doing it now?' She asked the question in an uncharacteristically nonchalant, uncaring manner which made me suspect that the answer mattered a great deal.

'Now? I'm not sure. Actually, I know what it was,' he said. 'I had this dream about a week ago, and we were all here with the van at the coast. Well I was, anyway. And a bottle washed up on the shore, with a message in, a message from the future. A bright blue little bottle it was, and I knew, the way you know in dreams, that the message was important. Really, massively significant. But I woke before I could read what it said. And thinking it over the next morning, it seemed like an indication that subconsciously I had unfinished business, that I had to do this. So I phoned up Will and remembered from meeting you at that party that you still had the van...'

He trailed off in mid-sentence. 'Actually, now I say that out loud, that makes a lot less sense than I thought it did.'

There was a short pause before Penny spoke. 'Did it look like that?'

She was pointing to a bright blue bottle that bobbed around in the surf of the gently breaking waves, a metre or so out to sea. From the way Russell's jaw flopped open, I deduced that it looked exactly like that. He pulled his hood over his head and ran through the pelting rain and across the shingle to the water's edge.

The bottle bobbed merrily in front of him, just out of reach. Russ glanced around for driftwood or anything that he could reach it with. Seeing nothing, he stepped out into the surf, quickly soaking trousers and shoes. He grabbed the bottle and ran back to the shelter of the van. He looked down at the bottle in his hands, staring at it in a shocked disbelief.

'That,' he said, 'is really fucking weird.'

I took a sip of my tea.

The bottle was about five or six inches tall, with a cork pushed half-way into the end. An inch or so of water was in the bottle, presumably deliberately, as this weighted the bottle enough to float in that pleasing upright manner. The glass was thick and a deep blue, but you could see that there was something inside: a scroll of paper.

I looked up from the bottle to Russ' face. The appearance of this bottle just after he talked about his dream was such an unlikely synchronicity that I wondered if it was set up. Could he have slipped the bottle into the sea earlier that morning? Christ knows why he would do that, but Russell is Russell and I've given up trying to make sense of the things that he does. But his face looked truly amazed, and perhaps a little scared.

'Are you going to open it?' I asked. He looked at me, seeming not to know what he should do.

'Be quick, before you wake up', said Penny, and her sarcasm snapped him out of his frozen state. He pulled out the cork and fished around inside the neck with a finger, then he dragged the scroll out of the bottle.

The scroll turned out to be piece of paper around A5 in size. At first I thought it had been laminated, but on closer inspection it turned out to be some strange, flexible plastic, beautifully printed in two colours and seemingly water proof. The three of us read it at the same time. This is what it said:

Chapter One:

1. In the beginning was the Word.

2. No-one knows what this Word was, or what language it was in, or whether it was said sarcastically or not. This is because the beginning was such a long time ago, and no-one who is around now was around then.

3. There are also no recordings of the Word available, which is a shame, as it would have made a good ring-tone.

4. Over the years, many people have claimed that they knew what the Word was. Some say that the Word was 'God'. Others, that it was 'funky', or 'artichoke', or 'jiggle'.

5. *The wise person says, 'This does not concern me. This Word, if ever there was one, was not intended for my ears.'*

6. *'I know this because I was not around at the beginning, and no-one would think to look for me there.'*

7. *'If anyone needs to speak to me I am quite contactable.'*

We read it, and we read it again, then we all fell silent.

There seemed to be a deep sense of disappointment emanating from Russell.

Eventually he spoke. 'What the hell is that?'

I looked at it again. 'It's the start of a bible.'

'A bible from the future!' offered Penny, with another noticeable splash of sarcasm. 'Does that make you a virgin or something?'

'But... what's the point of it?'

'Well, in your dream you knew it was significant. And what could be more significant than a brand new bible?' I wasn't very convincing, I knew, but I was doing my best. 'You've dreamt the coming of a new bible!'

'But it's a not proper. It's a joke version.'

I read it again. I quite liked it.

Russell rolled it up again and stuck it back in the bottle. 'What I don't understand is who would write... *that*, and go to the trouble of getting it printed up, and then throw it in the sea?'

Penny shrugged. 'Don't ask me. Throw it back and finish your tea.'

Russell pressed the cork back in. 'I don't mind admitting, Will, that I'm a bit disappointed.'

'You were expecting your dream message which washed upon this real shore to be of a higher standard, I take it?'

'I was, yes.'

'More... enlightening?'

'Yes. More enlightening would have been good.'

'Come on, before Penny drinks our teas.'

'Will – what should I do with the bottle?' When Russell was unsure of what he should do, he would often ask me like this, as if I was his parent.

'Chuck it back.'

'But it could be important.'

'Then I'll keep it. And if it doesn't get any more interesting, I'll throw it away later.'

He seemed pleased with this. 'Okay. Thanks.'

He handed me the bottle and picked up his tea.

3

We didn't see the sun that day. With both our headlights and windscreen wipers on full, and with sheets of water spraying out from our wheels, we skirted through Margate and drove back west. The biblical rain had no intention of easing. The awfulness of the weather seemed enhanced by the ugliness of the route. Industry and wasteland lined the roads. We weaved between the endless heavy goods vehicles which populated every spare yard of the A2. I have never been so pleased to see the Dartford Tunnel.

And yet, the atmosphere in the van was better. It may have been that the effect of a miserable September day in Kent made the ugliness inside the van seem relatively more endurable. I thought, though, that the three of us were getting used to each other again. As I drove through the colourless damp, I felt a spark of optimism.

It was certainly better than the previous day. Russ and I had arranged to meet Penny at nine in the morning. We had recently discovered that she still owned our old tour van, and Russ was adamant that this was the only vehicle that could be used for this journey. The plan was for Penny to bring the van down to Brighton, where I lived. She would then collect both me and Russ from Marine Parade, by the Palace Pier.

We arrived on time, clutching our backpacks and sleeping bags. At around ten o'clock she texted me to say she was running late.

By midday Russ had attempted to take the edge off his anger with vodka. The amount of time you take to drink a bottle of vodka is a major factor in the unpredictability of its impact. Suffice to say, Russ drank the bottle at an angry speed. There are times in your life when you can get away with drinking a bottle of vodka at an angry speed in the middle of the day, but they are in your early twenties. And also, in your late fifties. But definitely not around your fortieth birthday.

The thought of this journey and the return of the van seemed to be causing Russ to regress into a version of his younger self, back to when he had cheekbones and potential. This was not going to end well.

When Penny finally arrived, at close to two in the afternoon, it was unlikely that he would have spoken to her even if he had been coherent enough to do so. He simply stepped up to the old Transit, spread his arms as wide as they would go, and attempted to embrace the van like a long-lost friend. Then he kissed the cold blue metal, slid open the side door and collapsed into the back. Looking out of the driver's window, Penny observed all this without comment. Then she adjusted her wild mane of hair, climbed out of the van, and flashed me a huge smile.

'Will!' she said, and crushed me with a huge hug. She smelt of soap and cigarettes. Then she stepped back and looked at me.

'Hello Penny', I said.

'Hello Fucknuts. Look at you, still wearing band t-shirts and jeans at your age. Well, you've still got the figure for it, I suppose. I see Russell is wearing the same clothes as before as well, but at least he has a reason to. Very slimming, those black polo-necks.'

'What's it been, eighteen years?' I asked, as you do at moments like that.

'Have I changed?'

I smiled politely.

'Yeah, I know what you're thinking. I'm starting to look like my mother, aren't I? That's the way it goes, I guess. The passing years make all girls grow to look like their mother. Whereas, the same years make all men look more and more like potatoes.'

She paused to give me time to notice the insult.

'I'm just lucky my mum is a Goddess, I guess. Are you staying put as some sort of art statement, or are you getting in the van?'

She drove us east, speeding along the A259 coast road, trying to make up for lost time. We passed through Newhaven, Eastbourne and Hastings, accompanied by contented snores from the back. The cabin of the van filled me with nostalgia. The dashboard was sparse by modern standards, a functional grouping of chunky plastic switches on a grey vinyl backdrop. It was a vehicle from a previous decade, badly worn and shamelessly unsophisticated, but still perfectly familiar. There wasn't a single digital display to be seen. I breathed in deeply and the smell of the vinyl whisked me back to younger days.

It hit me then that this journey was actually happening. It hadn't seemed quite real up until that point. But then, why would it? Nothing about it made any sense and it must be the least likely thing I have ever undertaken. But there I go again, favouring things that made sense over things that actually happen. That's always an easy trap to fall into. Almost without me, the journey had begun.

4

On the morning of the third day I woke early and noticed the silence. The rain had stopped. I was lying next to the van's side door, so I pulled an arm out from my sleeping bag in order to open the door and look outside. I found myself looking at a calm still sea and, at that exact moment, the sun rose. It appeared directly in front of me, a mark of the sweetest yellow emerging from out of the waters. I watched it for as long as I could, feeling immensely privileged in some way, until it grew too bright to stare at. Then I closed my eyes, and felt it on my face instead.

Penny and Russ were fast asleep so I pulled on my clothes and took a walk down to the shore. We were parked by some gentle dunes on the outskirts of Clacton-On-Sea, with the pier visible in the distance. Here, though, the beach was deserted, and I walked along the sand with only the gulls for company.

The previous night had been good. The rain had eased a little in the afternoon, but the evening was cold and drizzly so we sat in the back of the van and drank. The talk had been largely nostalgic, of our previous times in that van and especially the tour we did around the time of our first album. Those were good days. Somehow, the three of us had slept in that van with a PA system, amps, guitars and a full drum kit. We tried to work out just how that was possible. It wasn't possible, we all agreed. We must all be suffering from shared false memories.

Penny explained how she had bumped into Russ a month or so ago, at the 50th birthday party of the guy who owned a studio we used to record at. Apparently this was the night Russ remembered that we still had to make this journey. He had become increasingly insistent as he became increasingly drunk, and at one point had even managed to make the idea sound like it made some sort of sense. Russ always used to get excited about the idea of quests when he was drunk, I recall.

Penny, naturally, had agreed to his face while knowing full well that she had no intention of actually doing it. That was, at least, an aspect of their relationship that the intervening years hadn't changed. She didn't say what made her change her mind, though.

There was another blue bottle bobbing in the surf.

I stopped dead when I saw it. It looked exactly the same as the one Penny had spotted the previous morning, bobbing upright a few yards out. Amazed, I waded out and grabbed it. Once again it was corked, weighted with a little water, and contained a scroll. I didn't read it except to glance at the title at the top. It read, 'Chapter Two'.

I thought about this as I took my prize back to the van. The two bottles were found many miles and a whole day apart. What must the odds have been, I wondered, of them being found by the same people? And in the correct order as well? They were too high. Much too high. It was impossible. Yet there was the bottle.

Back at the van, Russ and Penny were still sleeping. So I sat down and read the contents of the bottle. This is what they said:

Chapter Two:

1. In the beginning there was a sort of formless void or nothingness, like the feeling you get when you wake up enough to be aware of yourself, but not enough to realise how hungover you are.

2. In this formless void, there were no pens, or paper, or word processors, or mouths, or ears, or language, or anything much to talk about.

3. Really, if you buy into the whole 'Beginning was the Word' thing, you have to assume that it was more of a thought than a word.

4. Many people have had a lot to say about the thinker of such a thought.

5. The Ancient Egyptians, for example, called this thinker Atum, and claim that he was lonely, and masturbated, and in doing so ejaculated what we now call the Universe.

6. Muslims, Christians and Jews tell a story that is essentially similar, but they give their thinker a different name.

7. And they insist that even though their thinker was male, and alone, and no-one was watching, he would never have had a wank.

8. That's just not the sort of God He was; they are very certain about this.

9. *The wise person says, 'I do not know how the Universe came to be.'*

10. *'But I'm pretty sure it wasn't my fault.'*

11. *'It's a good Universe in many ways, don't get me wrong, but I wasn't there when it started and you can't blame this one on me.'*

I read it two or three times, then put it back in the bottle. I knew that Russ and Penny would dismiss it for the same reasons they did the first chapter, as something that was not sufficiently serious. But I quite liked it. I started to wonder about Chapter Three.

5

Later that afternoon, after passing through Suffolk into Norfolk, we went for a walk along the long shingle spit towards Blakeney Point. The spit itself is three and a half miles long and ends with a nature reserve. None of us has a particular interest in wildlife or bird watching, but a long walk is an attractive option when you've spent three days in a van. There was little wind, and North Sea was calm and grey. It was almost as flat as the land.

I had been surprised by how isolated many of the little coastal villages we had passed through were. The rules of our journey dictated that we had to always take the nearest 'A' Road to the coast, but this was proving to be much more complicated and time consuming than we had first thought. Navigating around rivers like the Stour and the Orwell, for example, had taken us on a tortuously slow, indirect route, and it had shown us how geographically separated the little towns we found were from inland centres like Ipswich or Bury St Edmunds. Often there was just one road that joined them to the rest of the country. Before the coming of the car, they may well have been foreign countries.

Penny strode off ahead and Russ took the opportunity to take me to one side. 'Will', he asked, 'why is Penny carrying a spade?'

It was a good question. Penny marched on ahead with a garden spade in her left hand. It was a hefty tool, weighty and awkward to carry. I watched to see if she intended to use it as a walking stick, but instead she swung it upwards and carried the weight on her shoulder.

'I don't know', I answered.

'I find it a little weird'.

'It is a little weird. You ask her.'

'I'm not asking her.'

'I'm not asking her either', I said. I sensed that I would be happier not knowing.

'Do you think, if neither of us ask her about the spade, that she will explain it herself, when the time was right?'

I thought about this. 'If I was carrying a spade, I would most definitely refer to it sooner rather than later, whether I was asked to or not.'

'Me too', agreed Russ. 'Let's not mention the shovel. Come on.'

We hurried on and soon caught her up.

'It'll be good to get back to the mainland', I said, meaning it would be good to leave East Anglia and get past the Wash. Penny nodded, understanding exactly what I meant. This marshy, sparsely populated outcrop feels separate to the rest of England. Russ stopped and pointed out to sea.

'All that used to be land, you know? Land all the way to Holland and Denmark. Thousands of years ago, I mean.'

'Eight thousand, or a little less,' added Penny casually. Penny was a geography teacher, although I was always surprised when I remembered that. For a geography teacher she is far more rock n' roll than me or Russ.

'This is where people first came to Britain, most likely. This was the very place where they arrived', Russ said. 'Imagine my great-great-great-grandfolks trekking this way on foot, exploring the west, following the setting sun to find out where it went to each night.'

'Maybe. Maybe not,' said Penny. 'They more likely came in boats at a later time. I like to imagine your ancestors being brought here as slaves. In a cage with a few pigs.'

'You imagine what you like. I'm imagining great explorers following the sun.'

I turned and looked at Penny. 'What happened to the land, then?' I said. I was making a point of recognising her as the expert among us. Russ was unlikely to extend that courtesy to her, so I felt that it fell to me.

'Probably a gradual thing. The land got swampier and swampier as sea levels rose at the end of the Ice

Age', she said. 'Then the floods came and the land bridge went. Some people think there was a massive land slip in Norway, and a giant Tsunami annexed Britain in hours. Imagine that. Imagine there were villages or towns out there. That land bridge was like an umbilical cord, connecting us to the continent. It fed these islands with animals and people, plants and trade. So when the cord was cut, East Anglia became the belly button of the island.'

'Ha!' Russell seemed delighted. 'Belly button, that's great. I knew there was a reason why I like this place. East Anglia is the British belly button. And it's an outy.'

'I don't know what it is about outy belly buttons, but they're funny. They are undignified. They are not sexy. They are odd and they look strange, but they have this bloody-minded lack of shame. 'Laugh if you want', they say, 'I am what I am'. They're like the people of East Anglia, basically, or at least how they are seen by the rest of the country.'

Russ stepped up to the edge of the water and addressed his next comments to the sea.

'I like this place, this flat, deserted coast. I like the miles of marshland where you would normally expect a beach. I like the way the tides have a wilful disregard for geography, and how it's impossible to be certain what is land and what is sea. The dualistic mind doesn't apply here, you know? There are places along these flatlands where the twenty first century hasn't arrived yet, and places that will never see the twenty-second. East Anglia is funny, but it is also epic, and anything that is funny and epic at the same time can't be a bad thing.'

He then turned back to see if me and Penny were impressed by his monologue. When he noticed that we'd wandered off, he didn't look too pleased.

'Hey this is weird. Where did this come from?' said Penny. She was peering down at a small starfish that she had found on the shingle near the surf. Russ frowned as he hurried along the beach to catch her up.

Intrigued, I looked closer at the starfish and saw that it was a plastic toy.

'It's plastic,' I told her.

'Yes I can see that it's plastic thank you. It's more that it wasn't there a moment ago, and now it is.'

She bent down, left her spade on the beach and picked the starfish up.

Me and Russ looked at each other.

'It probably just washed up from the sea,' said Russ.

'It's bone dry,' said Penny.

I watched Penny as she studied it closely. I could suggest that she was mistaken, that she simply hadn't previously noticed the small toy among all the pebbles and sand. It didn't seem worth the argument however. So I said nothing, and after a while she lost interest and hurled it out to sea.

6

That night Penny announced that Russ and I would be sleeping in the tent, and that she would sleep in the van. The tent was pitched in a field somewhere outside King's Lynn. When we settled down in our sleeping bags, we realised what her motivation was. Most of the ground was sodden from the rain, so the tent had been pitched on the highest part of the field where the ground was stony and uneven. We shifted about endlessly trying to find some comfort. Eventually I managed to contort my body into a shape that approximated the contours of the ground, and I lay there trying to remain as still as possible. Russ, however, was less lucky. 'Tomorrow night, we're getting a B&B,' he announced. I didn't argue.

'I'm coming round to the fact that Penny's with us,' he said out of the blue. 'I'm not annoyed at you for inviting her anymore.'

This was a little unfair, to say the least. I had not invited her along. She had invited herself. Russ phoned me out of the blue and suggested 'taking that trip that we used to talk about in the band,' so I had assumed that he would ask her as well, especially as he thought she still had the van. But then, I also assumed that she would turn us down.

'I think it's good that Penny's come,' Russ continued. 'It's a diversionary thing. It keeps my mind off my problem with music. I'm not sitting in the van obsessing over the fact that the radio isn't on. I'm sitting in the van worrying what she's doing here, which is far more confusing. Why has she come? It doesn't make any sense.'

It seemed a little late to worry about this not making any sense, but each to their own. I was more confused by what I was doing there than by Penny's motivation. That, I thought, was fairly clear cut.

'She's come along because of you, Russ, it's not rocket science.'

'But that would be a reason, not to come, surely? We're not friends, you know. We haven't spoken in a long time. It didn't end well. Surely the last thing she wants is to be stuck in my company again after all these years.'

I couldn't work out if he was being deliberately dumb or if he was trying to instigate a long, detailed conversation about how terrific he was. Either way, I had no choice but to play along.

'You're her first love, Russ, it's always going to be weird. If she was just an ex, that would be fine. Everyone understands what a relationship with an ex is like, good or bad, bitter or friendly. But when it's your first love, as it were, your high-school sweetheart, then it's a very different thing. You don't really know how you're supposed to relate to that person later in life. If you have any form of relationship with them at all, I mean. Mostly people just keep apart. Maybe there's a better way but if there is I don't know about it.'

This is the problem with camping. You don't have a television, so you end up having conversations like this instead.

'Think back to puberty,' I said to him. 'Remember what it was like when all those new experiences hit you? Emotionally, I mean, I'm not talking about the physical stuff. That whole shift of thinking when you become part of a couple, and you voluntarily surrender your sense of yourself as an individual and become part of something else? Do you remember that? Well, our formative experiences of those emotions are what shape our relationship with them from that point on. 'Imprinting', it's called. Our brain has encountered something new. It has to come up with some way to catalogue what has happened, so it wires itself up based on those first experiences. And those experiences, in her case, are shaped by you, by your personality and how you reacted to her.'

'Fast forward a few years, and you're no longer together. She meets all these new interesting men and starts relationships with them. And when she gets close to someone new, her brain then recognises what is going on. It thinks, 'Ah, I know this', because it has all this wiring that describes the relationship of a couple.

But that wiring, it's still based on you and your personality, and her new partner is a completely different person. Hopefully. So what does her brain do? Well, it does the best that it can. It tries to fit that person into the existing model of the relationship with you. There will be some new aspects of that new person that don't really fit, and it will try to incorporate those into its model in some way. But often, for simplicities sake, it will misinterpret them slightly. Or try to force them into the original wiring, even though they're the wrong shape, as it were. Then there will be aspects of her new partner that are completely new, totally unlike you, but because they're not understood by the wiring she'll tend to just not notice them. There will be aspects of this new person that she just won't pay attention to, because her brain isn't expecting them.'

'And then there are aspects to you that are unique to you, which other men won't have. But she's got all these neurons linked together which describe that aspect of relating to you and understand it as part of the couple relationship. They just sit there, these pathways, unused and withering away, but they leave her with a sense that her new relationship is not quite enough, that something's missing. This is what I mean when I say that she'll never be totally free from you. You'll always be part of her, a founding part of her life like a childhood illness or an inspiring teacher. And of course that part of her brain, how she interprets relationships, that's not a static thing. It's constantly changing and being rewired and improved, and it learns from new partners and experience. But it evolves; it doesn't wipe the slate clean and start from scratch. The foundations will always be you, no matter how deeply buried they become. Do you get that?'

He took a second to consider my words before he announced his judgement. 'That's total bollocks,' he said.

I tried again.

'Think of it like the London Underground if it's easier,' I said. 'It does change over the years, the Jubilee line gets extended and the East London line gets shut down, but this is just tinkering around the edges. The main design is too integral to be seriously changed. So your first love is not like a typical ex who you can put behind you. They'll always be part of you. Not a particularly useful part, admittedly. More like a low-level failure of judgement, making you get people a little wrong and ruining your chances of happiness. That sort of thing. But you can't complain because they are intrinsically you. Or maybe you're intrinsically them, I'm not sure.'

I trailed off, tangled up in my own metaphor.

'It's an interesting theory and all, Will, but you're not talking about Pen. You're talking about yourself. Or me. Or men in general. Let's agree that that's the case for men. But women? Women are over their first loves. It's not an issue. And believe me, if that wasn't the case we'd know about it. They wouldn't shut up about it. But women have processed their first love. They've moved on. Because they can do that sort of thing, you know. They have emotional powers that we men are just too backwards to understand. Like superpowers. They use those powers to repair themselves, in a way men can't. You know all that wailing and freaking out? That's what that's about. They are reforming their synapses. They are closing down the Central Line, to use your analogy, and building a shiny new monorail between White City and Bank.'

'But that's not the half of it. Yeah yeah, think it through. Your simplest, most stereotypical start to relationships goes like this: a teenage boy and a teenage girl hit puberty, and they respond by coupling up, say for a couple of years. That's about the norm.'

'Not for me it wasn't,' I said.

'I'm generalising. Don't dismiss generalising, it can be very helpful. Generally speaking. Now, there's nothing on Earth like the love of a teenage girl for a teenage boy. I mean its borderline insane, it's a physical thing. It's painful. It's proper nuts. I've wondered why this is, and I can only assume that its nature's way of compensating for the fact that teenage boys are fucking idiots. They are all morons, the lot of them, and this might have caused the human race to die out had

Mother Nature not robbed teenage girls of any sense of reason or perspective. They love teenage boys so blindly that it doesn't matter how awful they are.'

'Now, these intense first relationships aren't going to last. The boy is so freaked out by the intensity of the girl that he wants to escape, or the girl wants a boy to live up to the pedestal that she has put him on. Either way, these things rarely last beyond the teenage years, which is all well and good. The woman learns not to love so deeply, to keep her distance, and she becomes wiser and more alluring and more marvellous. But the boy, he not only learns nothing but he assumes that what happened was normal, because that relationship is all he knows. He thinks, 'well, the fact that I was worshipped must simply be because I am *exceptional*. I'm some kind of rock star poet.' And, he assumes, other women will think so too. So he goes through life, relationship after relationship, not being worshipped by saner, wiser women, and eventually cracks at some point in his forties. He has his mid-life crisis and tries to fuck girls that are far too young for him, just because they might activate that poor withering collection of neurons that still think being worshipped is part and parcel of a healthy relationship.'

'So, back to me and Penny. It should be me that's behaving all freaky. It's me who should be weird. But as luck would have it, I'm too self-absorbed and shallow to care about how integral to my emotional wiring she is. And she's too far gone through her life to give a shit about us twenty years ago. In fact, I'd go further than that. Her brain will now be rewired to the extent that she not only doesn't really remember what we had, she physically cannot remember. The wiring that experienced us is no longer there. She is incapable of replaying how it was. All of which brings us back the question, what is she doing here?'

I made a sound, one more uncertain than uncommitted.

'You could always ask her,' I suggested.

'What, are you crazy? This is Penny we are talking about here. She thinks that conversation is foreplay before battle. Life's too short to risk talking to her or something as dangerous as that. No, we need to find out what she's doing here. Without asking her.'

I took the only sensible option at that point, which was to fall asleep.

7

In the morning I was woken by the tent around me being dismantled. Russell and Penny fussed at me, indicating that we should have been on the road by now. Evidently I had overslept. I pulled on my boots and did my best to greet the day. If there had been an early morning pot of coffee brewed, it had already been drunk and the pot packed away.

Then it hit me. We weren't by the coast.

'Where's the sea?' I asked. Russ pointed down in the direction of the bottom of the field. 'About half a mile that way. Why?'

'We've got to go look,' I told him. 'Come on!'

'We've got to get on the road Will', he replied.

'But the bottle! We've got to look for today's bottle!' I was still not properly awake and I assumed that this would seem reasonable.

'There's no bottle. Get in the van.'

'You'll see plenty of sea today, Will', Penny chipped in, 'and tomorrow and for weeks to come.'

'Are you not coming with me?'

'Just get in the van Will.'

I turned and ignored him. Neither of them called out as I made my way down the field. Neither made any effort to follow me either. I found a worn path along the hedge which took me in the direction that I wanted to go. It was not the best route, as it turned out, and the path quickly turned into a mud-bath. My pace slowed down as my progress demanded all of my limited concentration. The placing of each footstep became an important decision. The walk became more of a dance, with the normally-passive ground taking an active role and becoming my partner. A half mile can take a long time on ground such as this. Once or twice my partner tried to take away my boot, like a deranged Prince Charming searching for his Cinderella, but I was too quick and graceful for him. I hopped, shimmied and squelched my way down the field.

Eventually I came through a copse and found the coast. Or rather, I found the edge of a cliff, with a small bay below me. The sea was a pale blue that blurred into an identical sky. To my right I could see headland getting lower, trailing down to what seemed to be a small town built around a river mouth. But looking down at the coast made it clear that there was no way to get safely down. Instead, I scanned the water below. If there had been a blue bottle waiting for me I would have seen it, but there was nothing.

With that realisation, I suddenly knew how foolish I was being. This is never a nice feeling, and so far the passing of years has failed to take the edge off it.

There was nothing else to do but to turn around and make the uphill dance through the mud up to my no-doubt unhappy fellow travellers. Each step was unpleasant. Back at the van, I didn't say anything to them and they didn't say anything to me. I simply climbed into the back of the van, and Russ drove us on our way.

8

'School starts back today,' remarked Penny apropos of nothing.

We were on the A165, somewhere between Hull and Scarborough. The roads were straight and fast, and we were heading north up the east coast. We were making good time. I had initially been a little stiff from sleeping on the floor, but a gentle calm had descended on the van as the miles passed and my aches had faded into a general dull calm. The fact that the radio was switched off was starting to feel normal. No-one had spoken for many miles.

It took me a moment, but I slowly realised that Penny had said something odd. I tried to work out what was odd about it.

'What's that Pen?'

'School. It's the start of the autumn term today. New school year.'

I nodded. Still, I was aware that I was missing something.

Russ worked it out. 'So... are you not working this month?'

'No I'm not,' she replied in a matter-of-fact tone. 'I was fired.'

And with that the awkward atmosphere returned to the van, and settled.

'It's a shame really. I was good at the job. I enjoyed it. My Dad had been very proud of me when I started there.'

Russ and I had been so focused on why Penny had come on this trip that it hadn't occurred to us to wonder *how* she had been able to. I knew that she worked at a private school, so I may have vaguely assumed that her term times and holidays were different. Of course, I was in no position to make this journey either until a few days before we set off. Somehow a hole had appeared in my commitments and before I knew what I was doing I had taken advantage and slipped through. Because everything about this journey was so unlikely I think I had assumed that Penny's circumstances would have been equally unusual. If I was there, it didn't seem that unreasonable that she would be too.

Bowing to the inevitable, I supplied the line that she was waiting to hear.

'What happened?'

'Well, fucknuts here gave an interview to the music press, in which he told a lot of anecdotes about the drugs and the excesses of the old days. Then the parent of one of my pupils recognised me.

'Did he ask for your autograph?' asked Russ, a little hopefully.

'No, he showed the magazine to the headmaster.'

Penny waited for a reaction, but both me and Russell stayed silent.

'This led to a very awkward conversation with the headmaster, in which he enquired whether or not I had left certain relevant information off my CV, and if I had previously been the musician who went under the pseudonym 'Penny Fuckhammer'.

'Ah', said Russ.

'He then produced the magazine and showed me a particular photo, which I think you must have given the journalist Will. It was one where I was backstage half-naked with the words 'I love speed' written in lipstick across my tits.'

She was quite right, I had given a journalist a whole pile of old photographs, and that was one of them.

'The headmaster asked me point-blank if the young lady in the picture was me. I considered lying but my hair in the photograph looked so great that I had to claim it. And that, it seems, is enough to end a teaching career.'

I knew that it was not mine or Russell's fault that Penny had decided to adopt the name Penny Fuckhammer after our band broke up, or that she had a habit of writing pro-drugs statement across her tits. She knows her own mind and she can't be talked out of things like that. But I also knew that this not a good time to discuss personal responsibility. I remained quiet, and hoped that Russ would say something that would make everything okay. Surprisingly, he did.

'Yeah. Your hair did look really great in that picture.'

She turned to him and smiled.

'Ah, thanks babe.'

I kept my eyes on the road.

9

We spent that evening in Whitby. Russ was as good as his word and treated the three of us to a B&B for the night. We checked in and headed to our fresh, clean rooms for much needed showers.

Afterwards we met in the bar and debated how to spend the evening. Russ suggested that we head out and find another pub, one not quite as dead as the hotel bar, but a little dead on account of not having a jukebox playing music. I shied off, however, pretending that I needed an early night. I thought that he and Penny needed to spend a bit of time together and that I should do the decent thing and get out of their way.

Russ was clearly eager for a night out. He had changed his black polo neck for another, slightly cleaner black polo neck, and had at some point applied guyliner to his slightly booze-bloated middle-aged face. I'm not sure what the age limit for the wearing of guyliner is, or whether he had crossed it, but Whitby has attracted its fair share of ageing Goths over the years so I didn't think that anyone would complain. Penny had made some attempt to tie her hair back, but had kept on the same loose dress, jacket and boots she had been wearing that day. I watched the pair of them head out through my bedroom window, Penny nonchalantly swinging her spade as she walked up the road. Then I pulled on my boots and headed out for a walk.

Outside it was dark and cold, and the wind was steady. I wandered through the old streets towards the North Sea. It would have been hard to do otherwise, for the lanes and hills seemed to funnel everything towards the coast. This was a true, working port town, and it felt very different to Brighton, where I live. Brighton seems to have its back to the sea; it's so busy and active that it almost forgets that the water is there. The sea felt like everything here. The town only exists to serve it.

The streets were mostly deserted, which made what figures there were seem suspicious and threatening. Of course, that would be how I would appear as well, a stranger with a strange purpose. I strode along the streets on the north side of the River Esk towards the western harbour wall. The sound of the waves grew louder and my footsteps were the only noise to challenge them.

I soon came to the entrance to a narrow metal walkway above the breakwater, which left the land and disappeared into the darkness beyond. There was a gate that looked as if it should be locked at night, but which had been left open. I felt like I was being invited through. I peered along the breakwater into the darkness to see if anyone was there, but I couldn't see or hear another living soul. Wrapping my coat around myself I walked through the gate, into the wind and darkness, and followed the metal walkway as it curved out to sea.

I enjoyed this part of the walk. It was a feeling that I knew well, the feeling you get walking at night after a beer. I felt immortal and monumental. The wind was getting strong now, and I enjoyed that also.

At the end of the walkway I found an open trapdoor in the metal floor with a ladder leading down. Looking through the hole into the darkness below I could just make out the concrete seawall which supported the metal walkway. I was in no mood to turn back, so I climbed down.

The concrete wall was no more than half a foot above sea level. It was only a couple of meters across and there were no guide rails or safety fencing. Despite the metal struts supporting the walkway above my head, I felt exposed. The water lapped against the stone and splashed sporadically over it, wetting my boots. Standing at the edge, I realised that this was the end of my walk. There was nowhere to go from here, other than back.

I turned around and looked back toward the shore, surprised at how far away the lights were. It was a cloudy, moonless night, and while I could just make out the ruined abbey on the south hill there was nothing between that and me but solid darkness. I could no longer hear anything but the sea all around me. I found a raised part of the concrete which was dry, and I sat down on this cold hard seat. I looked out at the water but only saw more of that perfect darkness. I wrapped my coat around myself as tightly as I could.

Time passed. The earlier excitement withdrew, my thoughts slowed down and what remained was a dull boredom.

What was I doing here, I wondered? What events had transpired to bring me here, cold and alone, sitting in pitch darkness somewhere off the north-east coast? Could I honestly see any point in this journey? Why was I doing it? I must have seemed like a good idea once, but it did not look that way now.

I thought about where I would rather be instead, but there wasn't anywhere that came to mind. No building or town or family that felt like home, no vocation or work that I felt needed undertaking. I had been married, happily, but my wife had died nearly three years ago. It was possible that I was still in shock, or at the very least still numb. It didn't seem that way to me, though. It wasn't that I was unable to feel anything. It was that there wasn't anything to feel.

But that is okay, I reminded myself, this is how things are. There is something comforting about a brutally honest appraisal of events, knowing that you are not blinded by optimism or false hope. It is only slipping away from that cold sober reality that scares me.

I thought of being stuck in the van for the next three weeks with Penny and Russ and the tension that they create, and I sighed. Why had Penny come along, I wondered again? Had she some hope of getting the old band back together? There were forums on the internet where a handful of people talk obsessively about just that, but that talk is deceptive. I was the only one of us still working as a musician, and from my dealings with tour promoters and record companies I haven't seen any desire for the old band to get together again. As a one-off, possibly, if the excuse was right, but there would be no future in it. We wouldn't be able to make a living.

And that was the problem, wasn't it? After the band had broken up I had started working as a session drummer. I had found enough studio and tour work to keep my head above water. But recently I've found myself becoming sloppy. My timing is not what it was. I've started making mistakes live. No-one had said anything, but I know they have noticed. Already the work is getting more sporadic. In part I wonder if I am doing it on purpose. The problem, to boil it down, is that I no longer know why I'm doing it.

When you are too close to something, you don't always notice the long, slow, drawn out slide into the inevitable. But you'll notice eventually, and sitting out there in the cold, black void, I could see it then. I could see it stretching back and back. How far back did it stretch, I wondered? At what point had the engine stalled and the cruising begun?

Never mind. It was all in the past. I tried to shift my thoughts to the future and found that I could not imagine one. The future was as blank as the night around me. What could I do, an ageing drummer whose heart is no longer in it? A widower with no appetite for a replacement wife or family? A man on the end of a breakwater off the North Yorkshire coast in the depths of night, because there is nowhere else he should be?

None of this bothered me unduly. I felt strangely content. I shifted my weight against the cold metal pillar and attempted to wrap my coat even tighter around me. I thought about what Celine would have said about me ending up there. That was my wife, her name was Celine. Her reaction made me smile. Gradually, I drifted off into a deep sleep, oblivious to all that surrounded me and all that was to come. Yet I think that, at some point in the night, a faint *chink chink chink* entered my dream. It was the tap of glass against stone, as a small blue bottle floated up from the darkness of the North Sea and knocked against the concrete breakwater that was my bed.

10

I returned to the B&B the next morning and found Russell eating alone in the small breakfast room on the ground floor. I squeezed into the pine chair next to him and ordered a full English breakfast.

'Where's Pen?' I asked. He shrugged.

'Not sure. Probably not up yet.'

'Late night, was it?'

'Not for me,' said Russ. 'Don't know about her. I came straight back but she stayed out.'

'She stayed out?'

'She was determined to drink.'

'Ah, okay,' I said. 'Did you two not have a drink then? I thought you'd been getting on better.'

'We've been getting on fine. It turns out that there are pubs that have no music playing, but they're not the type of pubs that let you in if you're carrying a spade.'

'Is that right?'

He nodded. 'It turns out, a spade can be considered a weapon.'

I thought about this.

'It's not a very practical weapon though, is it?'

'It's not a practical weapon, no', he agreed. 'In terms of carrying it about. But the barman's point was, you could do a lot of damage with a spade.'

'Well, technically, yes. But it's a judgement call, isn't it? Deciding which people in your pub are the type to use a spade as a weapon, I mean. Surely Penny isn't that sort of person?'

'We probably shouldn't think about that too much,' suggested Russ.

We both went quiet.

'Could she have, perhaps, not taken the spade with her?'

'We didn't discuss that option as fully as I would have liked,' admitted Russ. 'She was firmly of the opinion that she was going to carry the spade, so that was the end of the matter.'

I nodded. He went back to sliding a chunk of wrinkled sausage around the plate, collecting the brown sauce and the egg yolk as he did so. Russ ate like a man who is delighted that he has put on a few pounds and is hoping to put on a few more.

'Anyway, look at this,' I said, producing the blue bottle I had found by the end of the breakwater when I woke. Russell rolled his eyes.

'No but look,' I continued, fishing the paper out of the bottle. 'This isn't Chapter Three. It's Chapter Seventeen. It's like we missed a load of them when we came up the east coast so fast.'

I tapped at the top of the page where it stated 'Chapter Seventeen'.

'Let's have a look at it then', he offered. I turned it to face him and put it down on the old wooden table, next to his breakfast. He took a slurp of tea and read:

Chapter Seventeen

1. Beware of the man with one religion, for he understands nothing but he does not know that he understands nothing, and he will get in the way and cause all sorts of trouble.

2. Beware also the woman with no religion, for they are clinging to a very specific semantic definition in order to avoid hard questions. They are fooling no-one! Except themselves.

3. Beware also the person with a dozen religions, for they are confused and bamboozled, and in danger of losing the plot, and will not be much use in a crisis.

4. The most practical and useful approach is to have three religions.

5. I mean, roughly three. It's not an exact science. But between two and five, something like that.

6. Three is good though. You can position yourself in the centre of three religions and in doing so drink of their wisdom without falling for their bullshit.

7. Choose three religions that you like, obviously. Three that speak to you as an individual. Don't just go for the popular ones for the sake of a quiet life. It doesn't work like that.

8. Consider the man who is a Daoist, a Pagan and a Christian. Consider the woman who is a Buddhist, a Sikh and an atheist. These people won't easily fall for your nonsense. These people will have a wide perspective. These people will be able to get on in life.

9. These people are also unlikely to start wars, or proclaim certainties on street corners, or spit at people they don't know. They will also be easier to seat at weddings.

Russell finished reading and shrugged.
'So I don't know what to do,' I said. 'About the missing chapters, I mean.'
'Do? What can you do?'
'Well that's just it...'

'Will, we're not going to drive back down the coast looking for bottles you missed, you know?'

I nodded.

'Yes. Of course. That would be crazy, wouldn't it? That would be a properly crazy thing to do.'

'I think so.'

My breakfast arrived. I started to butter the toast. Russell neatly placed his knife and fork along the centre of his now-empty plate, and stood up.

'I'll go and wake Penny while you eat that. I'm looking forward to today, actually. Goodbye England, hello Scotland.'

I watched as he left the room, then rolled chapter seventeen back up and put it back into its bottle. Only then did I notice that he had left his black notebook on the table. I ate the last of my sausage as I debated whether or not to look inside it.

Russ is a writer now. Or at least, that's what he tells me, although I'm not aware of him actually writing anything. He is certainly no longer a musician. He had a solo career after the band split up, and was reasonably successful for a while. But he quit music five years ago, announced that he was a writer and, as far as I can tell, has done nothing but live off the royalties from his one big hit.

I put my knife and fork down and decided that yes, I was going to look inside his notebook. I opened it at page one and began to read.

11

IDEAS BOOK
Russell Douglas

Jan 1st.

A new year, a new notebook - here I'll note down any and all story ideas as I have them.

I have sold my guitar. I have dismantled my studio. I am no longer a musician. I am a writer now.

I will now write something.

April 6th.

NOVEL IDEA: Passport to Pimlico, but on the moon.

June 23rd.

NOVEL IDEA: King Arthur versus Robin Hood.

July 17th.

NOVEL IDEA: A version of *Hearts of Darkness* on a canal boat. Working title: *Fuck Off Death*.

August 10th.

Woke up with a name in my head - Orlando Monk.

October 31st.

Still struck by the name Orlando Monk. I feel he is the hero of a work of fiction. He is the ultimate protagonist. But who is he? What does he do?

OPTION #1:

Orlando Monk is an artist and a time-traveller. He is a sculptor, but his medium is time and his art is 'history'. He works in the background, unseen and unknown - a cross between Doctor Who and Banksy. His methods involve introducing certain people at certain times, or placing certain ideas in certain cultures, and in doing so he shapes drama and narrative, shock and surprise - he builds purpose and history out of chaos. He works on all scales, from the micro to the macro. He turns the history books from a dreamlike list of random events into narrative and (the illusion of) progress.

He is chameleon-like, a master of disguise. He speaks all languages and can copy any accent. His most identifiable trait, then is his height. At 5'3", he can not disguise his short stature (less a problem in past times, of course, when people were shorter).

He is totally amoral. His work impinges on millions of people - everyone, actually - and he cares not whether their lives are improved or ruined.

He is the first pretentious Trickster.

The art world of the future has great difficulty in correctly identifying genuine Monk's.

His motives are opaque.

November 5th.

The more I think about time travel the more I think it has been done to death. Story disappears into increasingly intricate and complicated paradoxes. Narrative starts to serve cleverness, rather than the other way round. Time travel stories are, ultimately, bullshit.

OPTION #2:

Okay, so there's no good reason why Orlando can't be a time traveller and an artist. He's a fictional character, after all. Fictional characters can do anything - or anything imaginable, anyway.

Which got me thinking: what hasn't been done already? What is imaginable, but which fictional characters haven't done yet? There have been characters that can fly like Superman, or have superhuman intellects like Sherlock Holmes. I need to find something like that, but fresh. And better.

Something new, something powerful, something cool.

Suggestion: a fictional character that has the power to step out of the world of fiction and into the material world. How? Because the fictional character was created with the ability to do so, therefore he can do it, QED.

After all, this is what ideas do, they emerge from the imagination and manifest in the physical world. Look around - what is there that you can see that was not first an idea? Objects, languages, culture - there is a boundary between the material and the immaterial worlds, but it is not fixed. The immaterial keeps crossing the line.

The immaterial are immigrants in the world of the material. No - they are colonists. They have taken over. It's their world now. What is left of this world that hasn't been shaped by the human mind?

What would a fictitious character make of the material world? What would he or she think of us?

Jan 11th.

Ah! Here we go, I've worked out Orlando Monk's backstory!

(Here a number of pages have been ripped out of the notebook)

February 29th.

The 'time travel' thing may not be so bad if you get rid of time machines and all that bullshit. Instead, do it this way: Orlando grabs his current point of time with one hand, and his intended destination with the other. He then draws them together, hops across, then lets them go - and they snap back into place. There's nothing else - nothing to find, nothing to hear, just two time points overlapping for a brief period when Orlando arrives, and leaves.

March 27th.
Struggling with the Orlando Monk book. Not getting anywhere.

May 1st.
Total writer's block.

May 9th.
REASONS NOT TO WRITE A NOVEL:
- Massive commitment in time, time that could be spent going to the beach or eating good food, etc.
- or indeed, time that could be spent earning a living.
- There is no money in it, no publishers advances anymore.

- There are too many novels as it is, the last thing the world needs is one more.

- endless chorus of self-published authors hawking their wares on Facebook, Twitter etc getting increasingly annoying.

- General sense of a stagnating artform, repeating itself rather than healthy and forward-looking.

- Sends you mad.

- Authors are wankers.

REASONS TO WRITE A NOVEL:

- To get the fucking thing out of my head.

- To show off.

- You've got to do something, man.

May 29th.

Feeling much happier now that I've made the decision to not write a novel and not be a writer. Starting acting classes on Monday.

May 30th.

Orlando Monk turned up at my house today. He was annoyed with me. He was really pissed off! He was banging on the door and...

--

Russ returned at that point looking for his notebook, so that's all I read.

12

'That's Holy Island?' said Russ. We were sitting towards the back of the bay, looking across the water at the Holy Island of Lindisfarne. 'It doesn't look that Holy to me.'

We had taken the A174 out of Whitby and driven past an endless string of golf courses around Middlesbrough and Hartlepool. Much of our route was urban and we passed through Sunderland and South Shields before we broke out into countryside once more. We had initially planned to stop at Whitley Bay but, confused by a sudden lifting of the cloud, we continued on to Holy Island instead. Unfortunately we had timed it wrong. Holy Island is a tidal island, and twice a day the high tide covers the causeway and separates it from the mainland. We had arrived during one such high tide and so, being unable to walk to the island, we sat and insulted it from a distance.

'It's a bit precious, isn't it?' said Penny. 'If you call it Holy Island, that's like saying that other islands are unholy. Which is a bit harsh.'

'I'm not sure,' I said. 'Have you been to the Isle of Wight?'

'It's the Christian boundary thing,' said Russ. 'Back in the dawn of time people would climb up a hill and turn through 360 degrees, and everything that they saw out to the horizon was sacred. Then later people would stick a church on that hill, and put a wall around that church, and the boundary would shrink from the horizon right down to that wall around the church. Inside that wall the land was still hallowed, but beyond the wall the world was now bad and scary and evil, full of Heathens and Trolls and people having a good time in unacceptable ways. All the goodness was gone. They called it 'unconsecrated ground'. It's a useful way to make something sacred, actually, you just declare everything else to be profane.'

'Does the causeway count as holy?' asked Penny. 'I mean, it's part of the island, but only at certain times of the day. Maybe it's only holy when the tide is out. Maybe the sea comes in and washes the holy off it. And then, when the sea goes away some angels come and stick the holiness back on.'

'The angel that ended up with that job must be pissed off,' I said. 'That's menial work. It's not the sort of work that wannabe angels dream of.' I was looking up the history of the island in a guide book, skimming over the details of illuminated manuscripts and Viking raids. It did seem that we were being unfair to this poor island. From the evidence of the guide book, it was more holy than the Isle of Wight. But I couldn't shake the feeling that its holiest days were long behind it and that it was living off its reputation. I used the potted history in the guidebook to support this prejudice, but in truth I based it on something far more suspect. I had looked in the bay, and there were no bottles containing pages from a future bible to be seen.

This might not be a system that many use but it was quite clear, to me, that this place wasn't as holy as it could have been.

Penny's words about the holiness of the causeway stuck with me that afternoon, as we drove up to Berwick Upon Tweed. The blue sky gave the coastal scenery a spring-like quality, and we were relaxed enough to spend long stretches gazing at it as we followed the road, not needing to talk. The question of where the boundary of Holy Island stopped and started seemed an apt one, considering our journey. Boundaries are strange things. You can only really see them from a distance. When you get close, they dissolve away into an indefinable grey area.

There is a fractal element to this, of course. We could have driven the length of this country in a day. We could have done a circuit of large cities – say London to Aberdeen, returning via Liverpool and Cardiff – in perhaps three days. The route we had chosen, in which we must always take the closest A road to the coast, would take us a month. If we had been more committed and insisted on driving on the closest road to the sea, it could have easily have taken six months. The greater the level of detail you use, the longer the journey would be. If you took a fine enough level of detail, including every crinkle in every rock, then the length of the British Coast would approach infinity. Getting too close to a boundary makes it shrink away from you.

But more importantly, the closer you get to boundaries the more arbitrary they appear. We were nearing Berwick Upon Tweed which, through complicated quirks of history, is currently the northernmost town in England as opposed to the Southernmost town in Eastern Scotland, although it has swapped sides a number of times over the years. What reason is there, in drawing the line above the town rather than below it? Would it have made a difference to the character of the place or the people who live there? I have never found the people of north east England to be that different from those in southern Scotland, but the people in south east England are distinctly different to those in the south west. And they, again, are very different to those from Yorkshire. If I'd been given the job of separating the north and south of this island into two separate people, the line would not be where it now stands. It would be somewhere else but, needless to say, that somewhere else would be equally arbitrary.

Wales does have a distinct identity, of course, but it is not as neatly contained as the map suggests. For a number of miles either side of the border, you cannot really say if the Welshness has begun or the Englishness ended. Get too close to the border and it dissolves away. Yet people want these clear-cut borders. There are those who base their entire identity on them, who would even kill because of them. How can people invest so much in such an arbitrary, random designation? Are we really that uncomfortable with a messy merging from one thing to another?

I suspect we are. Boundary areas are dangerous places. They are the areas after the previous rules stop and before a new system comes into play. They are liminal places, betwixt and between, places of uncertainty and unpredictability. They are thresholds. Perhaps there is a good reason why we just draw an arbitrary line on a map and then give it no more thought.

Why was I thinking about these things on that sunny afternoon, heading out of England? It may well have been the influence of the coast, that final boundary which shifts and surprises when you get too close. But I don't think that is the full story. I think I was aware that something else was happening to us. We had been away from normal life for five days now. It was fading from memory and seemed to have less and less hold on us. This journey was our life now, following the road, watching the moods of the sea. Reconnecting with the normal life, such as holding a conversation with a shopkeeper or phoning friends at home, was becoming increasingly difficult. Our journey didn't make any sense, so there was no way that those in normal life would be able to relate to us.

We had left normal life behind. Something else would take its place. But at that moment, in that boundary area, that something else had not yet become clear. And so we drove on, following the road around the coast, enjoying the sunshine whenever it chose to appear.

13

It was two days later.

I only asked the question to change the subject, really. We were tramping over a landscape called the Hill O' Many Stanes, just south of Wick on the north-east Scottish Coast. Russ was off in the distance, trying to look windswept and enigmatic. Rows and rows of dark megalithic standing stones, each the size of a small child, crossed the gorse and heather. Penny was trying to steer the conversation around to my late wife.

She had tried this a number of times over the previous week, but each time I had managed to avoid the subject. Penny should have understood, I thought. She knew me as a drummer and, like most drummers, I am not the communicative type. My silence about Celine should have made clear that I was not interested in discussing the subject. But there was a strange atmosphere to this place. It felt still, despite the cold wind coming in from the sea. It was not a melancholic stillness, even though the regular weathered stones could be likened to a graveyard. There was a sense of potential in the air, as if something new was growing underground and could burst forth at any moment. There was something about the atmosphere which might make Penny think asking me outright was a good idea.

'Why are you carrying that spade, Penny?' I had to ask something, for I could tell that she was moments away from asking me how I was doing. 'It's odd, you know, you carrying that big heavy thing.'

She looked down at it and seemed surprised, as if despite its weight she had forgotten that she had it. 'Oh this?', she replied. 'That's quite a good question.'

I said nothing and waited for her to continue.

'Sometimes you get a notion, you know? Just a strange little idea in your head that won't go away, that you can't shake? This was a few days before I met Russell again at that 50th party, actually. It was maybe a week before then but no more. Anyway, I was struck by this notion, that what Russell really needed was for me to smack him across the head with a heavy spade.'

I hadn't been expecting that. Or rather I had, but I hadn't been expecting to hear it spoken so plainly.

'A spade?', I replied.

'Yes, it had to be a spade.' Penny started judging the weight of the spade in her hands as if preparing to take a swing. I think it was a subconscious action, for her eyes were looking elsewhere as if hunting an earlier memory. 'Only a spade would do. Anything else wouldn't be right.'

'Well', I said in an overly cheerful manner, 'you'd knock him out cold with that!'

'Or kill him!' she replied. 'Which, obviously, I have no desire to do and obviously is something I'm not going to do.'

'No.'

'Even though, of course, you'd have a spade handy to bury him, so it would all work out. I'm joking of course. I'm far too together to go around killing people, you know that. Even people like Russell. Making their life hell is more my thing. But I was struck by this notion and it stayed with me, and then he asked me about the van. So I went out to my brother's garage to check on it and see if it still starts, and there, in his garage, was this spade.'

She held the flat end of the spade up, in front of my face, so that I could get a good look.

'And it's perfect, isn't it? It's exactly the sort of spade that you'd use if you wanted to crack Russell across the back of the head with a spade.'

'Which,' I added carefully, 'you don't want to do.'

'Absolutely! It would kill him, and that would be an awful thing to do. But as I say, I was struck with this notion and then he suggested the trip, and I had the spade, so it seemed silly not to come along and bring it. It would be for his own good, after all.'

'What? Being decked by a spade?' I asked.

'Yes. That's the important bit. What I was most struck by was that it would be a good thing for him. I've got no interest in braining him, really, there's nothing in it for me and it would cause all sorts of hassle. And I'm sure I won't do it. But you know how it is, when you get a notion for something and you can't shake it. There's usually some reason behind it, somewhere. You have to pay attention to things like that.'

'I suppose so.'

A sudden look of confusion crossed her face. She pulled her hand out of her trouser pockets and held it out. There was a small plastic starfish on her palm.

'Jesus,' she said. 'What's that doing there? I threw that away!'

'Or possibly, you put it into your pocket?' I added helpfully.

She was studying it intently.

'It's the same one! How is that? How can this be the same one?'

She brandished it accusingly in my face.

'Oh I hate that stuff, things moving about by themselves. No-one needs that. What's that about? It's hard enough staying sane as it is, without things moving about by themselves. I threw this away hundreds of miles ago.'

I made a sort of shrugging gesture, and considered finding a polite way to back away.

'You don't think Russell slipped it into my pocket, do you? To freak me out?'

'I don't think that that would be high on his To-Do list, no.'

'Right, I'm going to throw it away, and throw it away properly. Are you watching?'

I nodded.

'Good. You're my witness. Here goes...'

Penny hurled the small plastic starfish in an elegant arc through the air. It sailed across the hill and disappeared somewhere in the distance.

'Now I definitely threw that away, didn't I?'

I assured her that she did.

She nodded, satisfied, then picked up her spade and marched away.

14

The thin crescent of the new moon hung above me, fading slightly as the light increased. It would be full again in two weeks, I realised. I tried to work out where I would be then.

'You're up early', said Russ. I had heard him stirring in the van, and had stayed still and quiet in order not to wake him. It was a few minutes before dawn, and the first light was leaking over the horizon.

We had parked up on a cliff top overlooking the North Sea not that far from the Hill o' Many Stanes. We were at the far north east of Scotland. It would be the last time on the trip that the sea would be to the east, and hence the last time we'd see the sun rise out of the water. I had risen early to see it.

'I'm just waiting for the sun rise', I told him. 'Did I wake you?' He shook his head.

'No, I couldn't sleep that well. Are you staying up here? I'm going to clamber down.'

There was just enough light so I followed him down, climbing across the rocks until we came to a small patch of pebble beach. I sat next to him and we looked out to the east, waiting for the sun. In the chilled half-light the noise of the water running back through the pebbles dominated the scene, louder than the waves that broke over them. It was a strange sound, as the pebbles jiggled against each other for position as the wave left the shore. It was static imagined by stone.

'How are you getting on with Penny?' I asked. It was a conversation we would have to have sooner rather than later.

'Yeah okay... But you know...' He shrugged. I remained silent, making no effort to take over the conversation.

He looked behind him, making sure she hadn't left her tent and followed us down.

'It's just like...' he continued eventually, 'Okay, I accept that she's still got this thing for me, that's why she's here, and I'm being careful not to provoke that. On the surface it's fine. She's being friendly enough, you know, nothing's obviously weird about it. But there's nothing real about it, or at least it doesn't feel like there is. It feels like she's someone on Facebook, someone you once hung around with and have befriended on there for old time's sake. And you pass a few messages back and forth to be polite and that's fine, but it's not a real relationship, you know? No proper connection, for good or ill. It's like spending time with a record company person who is just there because it's their job. Do you know what I mean?'

I nodded, but I wasn't entirely sure that I did. I'm pretty antisocial and that sounded like a reasonable relationship to me.

'Because it's got me wondering. Is there a workable model where people like me and her can have a relationship that is in some way healthy? You get all these people getting divorced after tracking down their high-school sweethearts on Facebook, and confusing their memory of them with who they have become. Even worse, they can confuse their memories of themselves, their younger selves, with who they are now. Getting back together would never work, everyone understands that. We don't know each other anymore, but we sort of assume that we do. That's not a good combination.'

'But can we recognise that on some level we're important to each other? I'm thinking about Godparents, you know? The way that they are not parents, not related, have no reason to be involved, but they still look over the children. They're on their side. I'm wondering if there could be an equivalent, a sort of Godpartner? There's a certain intimacy and concern even though they're not your partner and they're not the focus of your life. But you do look out for each other in some way. What do you think? Do people work like that?'

I thought about the conversation I had had with Penny about the spade. 'I don't think that's a goer, Russ,' I said.

I looked out to sea. There was a thin layer of cloud on the horizon, but as the top of the sun broke through it seemed to dissipate. Then I heard a chink of glass tapping against stone, unmissable in the spaces between the withdrawing waves. I looked down at the blue bottle which came ashore by my feet. I picked it up and held it in front of my eye. It sparkled with deep golden highlights in this pre-dawn light and, at that moment, I don't think I could have imagined a more beautiful sight.

I fished the scroll out from the neck of the bottle and opened it quickly. I only read the first two words. They caused me to sit bolt upright, my face finding itself pointed straight at the emerging sun. 'Chapter Five', it had said.

Chapter Five. I hadn't been expecting that.

'What is it,' asked Russ, noting the shock on my face.

Chapter Five had come after Chapter Seventeen. They were not all in order. And if they were not all in order, then it no longer followed that I had missed any of the bottles.

And instantly, I knew what that meant.

I knew that I had not missed any chapters.

I knew that I would receive them all.

I knew that my future stretched out as clear and as defined as my past. As it always has done.

And the sun rose.

And at that moment, Penny's voice called from the top of the cliff. 'Russell! Will! You'll never guess who's up here!'

PART TWO: PENNY

Day 10 (Hill O' Many Stanes) - Day 24 (The Lizard)

15

'Russell! Will! You'll never guess who's up here!' I shouted.

For a few months during our final tour, we had hired a session guitarist and toured as a four-piece. This guitarist, it turned out, was a knob-head. He was a miserable sod and he nicked one of Russell's guitars at the end of the tour. His name was Graeme something-or-other. And I had just woken and found him peering into our van.

'Hello Penny!' he said, as if he had last seen me yesterday.

I stared back at him as I awaited the return of the boys. He had short cropped hair and his round face was paler than it should be. He was still recognisable as his younger self, though, apart from his epic beer belly which seemed to belong to someone else.

'Bloody hell, it's that bloke who stole your guitar!' muttered Will as he clambered back up the cliff top, pushing his greying curly hair away from his eyes to make sure.

'Hello Will! Long time!' waved Graeme.

Will stood a little distance away, rubbing his stubbly chin with the side of his hand and watching how Graeme acted. He seemed unsure as to whether he should enter into a conversation with him or not.

'I don't believe it,' said Russell, who followed Will up the cliff. 'It's Graeme!'

Graeme reacted more to Russell's voice than his appearance. 'Russ!' he called back. 'I didn't recognise you for a second. It's the bald thing, you know. How are you?'

The pair shook hands, a little formally.

'What are you doing here?' asked Russell.

'What am I doing here? Aye, that'll be right,' said Graeme to himself. 'This is where I am Russ. I'm just doing my thing, you know? I've not wandered into your story. You've wandered into mine. What you should be asking is, what are you doing here?'

'We're just, er...' Will began. He trailed off as he remembered that he didn't really know what we were doing there.

'We're on a journey,' said Russell.

'A journey? That's nice. Where are you going?'

'It's er, it's not that easy to explain.'

I spoke up. 'We're driving the van around the coast of Britain to see where we end up, even though where we end up will be where we started.'

Russell nodded.

'Oh that's nice,' said Graeme. 'So you're... sightseeing?'

'It's possible that that's what we're doing,' said Will. 'We're not entirely sure ourselves.'

'Just the three of you? In that old van?'

We nodded.

'You're not heading to Glasgow, by any chance?'

'We are,' said Russell cautiously, 'Eventually. But not via a very direct route.'

'Ah, you're a Godsend!' cried Graeme. 'What are the chances? I'll come aboard with you, and when we reach Glasgow I'll buy you all a meal in this nice little place I know, to say thank you.'

We all looked at each other.

'It's going to take us about 4 or 5 days to get there,' said Will.

'Perfect!'

'Why is that perfect? What's perfect about spending five days going to Glasgow the long way?'

'Why?' asked Graeme. 'Okay, I'll tell you what's going on here. You three have wandered into my story. Now what you're doing probably seems important to you, and that's nice. But my story is far more interesting, so it takes precedent. You understand? There are some friends of mine - well I say friends, they want to attack me with a hammer. And they are nearby, and I have to get out of here. I have to get to Glasgow, where there's a large amount of money that will make everything all good again. And if I could get to Glasgow without being found, by going the long way in your van, then I'd like that very much.'

Graeme beamed a huge grin at us all.

'You've messed up a drug deal, haven't you?' asked Russell.

'I have, yes.'

'Graeme I hate to break it to you but your story is rubbish,' said Russell. 'People messing up drug deals in this day and age - it's been done to death. It's tedious, man! What are you, eighteen?'

Graeme looked a little crestfallen.

'It's a bit more complicated than that,' he said. 'There's a woman, and a computer disk and all that sort of stuff.'

'That's even worse!' said Russell.

Deep down, I think Graeme knew he was right. 'How about, I don't insult your story, and you don't insult mine,' he said. 'Have we got a deal?'

'Sure.' Graeme and Russell shook hands again.

'You will, I assume, chip in for petrol?' asked Will.

Graeme smiled, and slapped him on the back. 'Will, look at it like this. There's your story, and there's my story. Your story is about driving along a windy road, and all that that entails. My story is about laying low for a few days, and hiding. Our stories will run alongside each other for a short while, but they are essentially separate things. You play your role, and I'll play my role.'

'You're not going to chip in for petrol then?'

'I'm not, no. That's your job.'

'Okay. It's good to be clear about these things.'

'It is, you're right,' he said. 'And there's one more thing we should be clear about. We should set off right now, and not hang around here any longer. Do you all understand that part?'

Will and Russell looked at each other, then they looked at me.

I turned to Graeme. 'We'd better get going then,' I said.

16

Hello, I'm Penny.

Before we continue, I'll tell you something about myself. It'll save time.

Life, for most everyone, is a lengthy exercise in standing up. This is not our natural state. Our natural state is to be curled up into a ball. If we could, we would assume a tight foetal position in a dark room that only we knew about, and just wait for everything to go away. That's the life we're designed for.

We can't do that, of course. We have hungers to satisfy and lives to lead. We stand and we go out into the world and we mingle with others. We expend energy constantly fighting this pull back to the foetal position, like an elastic band that must be kept stretched. But we're capable; we can do this. When we are young we possess vigour and when we are old we have perseverance, so if you forgive us the moments of disaster and illness when it is all too much, we keep standing.

You understand this, don't you?

But what I want you to know is, I'm different. That pull doesn't work on me. Standing tall is as natural as any other position. It's like that elastic band has snapped. Think of me as emotionally arthritic. I hurt but I don't bend.

You might wonder why I am like this. Have I always been this way? I have no time for questions like that. I don't care one way or the other.

Now you know that, I'll get on with it.

That night we parked the van in a layby on the A838, somewhere between Tongue and Cape Wrath on the Northern coast of Scotland. We were too tired to find a place to camp and, on this clifftop in this deserted wilderness, there didn't seem to be any point in looking. Russell, Graeme and Will were soon snoring in the back of the van. I lay across the seats in the front, covered in my coat, with a sweater as a pillow. The weather was too aggressive to bother pitching a tent, and I had slowly become acclimatised to the smell and the noises of the boys. There were no streetlights or houses for miles around so I could sleep without blacking out the windows. I watched the stars winking on and off between gaps in the cloud for a while, then I slept deeply.

I awoke with the dawn, stiff but rested. I sat up and was startled to see another vehicle in the lay-by. A red transit van was parked immediately in front of us, the two front bumpers facing and barely a foot apart.

Immediately I felt uneasy. It was unsettling to think that strangers had been around while I slept, and that they must have looked into the van and seen me out cold across the front seats.

I heard someone stir in the back so I turned, lent over the seat, and told the bodies back there to wake up as we had company. Russell, Graeme and Will responded by sinking back deeper into sleep.

When I turned back I noticed the plastic starfish for the first time. It hung down on a small chain from the red van's rear view mirror. A chill went through me. It was the same size and colour as the one I threw away earlier in the week. It swung slowly back and forth like a hypnotist's watch, even though the van was still and there was no-one in sight who might have knocked it.

It seemed a little cruel for the day to start messing with me so early. Nobody needs their sanity threatened before breakfast. I hoped this wasn't going to set a precedent. I threw an accusing glace back at the plastic toy, which swayed gently, innocent and nonthreatening. Then I opened the door and exited the van, determined to do something real and grounded. I was going to go and piss in the ditch.

I was halfway through when a voice to my left called, 'Morning!' I turned and saw a man pissing on the right rear wheel of the red van, smiling cheerfully at me.

'Morning', I said casually. The stranger was nearing six foot and thin. He had long straight hair tied back in a ponytail, and a scruff of hair on his chin that was probably once a goatee that had been left to run wild. He seemed remarkably relaxed about our meeting, as if I was another man having an early morning wee rather than a woman squatting in an ungainly fashion above a ditch with my arse in the elements.

'Lovely morning', the stranger offered. I mumbled my agreement as I buttoned up my jeans. I couldn't quite place his accent but it wasn't Scottish. Northern but not strong. Cheshire, perhaps? I wondered if he was the sort of person who was looking to attack Graeme with a hammer. My hunch was that he was not.

I had an overwhelming urge to ask him about the starfish but the thought of doing this made me nervous. The most likely outcome would be that he wouldn't understand what I was talking about. But what if he could explain what was going on, and the explanation was crazy? I didn't like the thought of that. Yet I had to say something to the man. We were the only waking souls for many miles and we had both shared an early morning piss by our vans, so the ice had been broken.

'You've got a plastic starfish suspended above your dash,' I said.

This comment caused the stranger to pause, and he finished and zipped himself away before responding. 'You're observant', he said at last.

'I saw a toy like that on the beach in East Anglia,' I continued. There was no point trying to make this sound reasonable. 'I couldn't work out how it had got there. Then I found it in my pocket a couple of days later. I threw it away.'

He nodded.

'It's not the most interesting of coincidences, perhaps, but I just wondered where you got yours from.'

The stranger laughed.

'Ha! Coincidence is it? You say you were in East Anglia, is that right? And you've driven up here?'

'Yeah.'

'You're driving round the coast, aren't you?'

There seemed to be an unstoppable momentum to this conversation and I could see no way to avoid it. I nodded slowly.

'I see', said the stranger, looking at me warily now. 'And how far have you come? How many laps?'

'Laps?' I instantly felt better. This man was clearly much madder than I was. 'We're not doing laps. We're just going around once.'

He smiled. 'Of course you are. Yeah.'

I was about to ask what he meant when a second figure appeared from his van. She was a tall woman in a black denim jacket, and was like the first stranger in being somewhere in that indeterminate age between adolescence and middle age. She rubbed the sleep from her eyes and looked at me.

'She's driving that van around the coast,' the man told her.

She looked back at me with a sudden interest. 'Is that right?' she muttered. 'How many laps?'

'She's still on the first. That's all she's planning to do.'

They both laughed.

'Of course she is,' the tall woman said, she and turned to me. 'A little helping hand for you. It's three times. That's the target, that's what it will take. But it won't matter, we've done two and a third circuits, nearly. We'll be the first to three.'

'I'm very happy for you' I offered.

'Maybe we could go in convoy', she continued. We're planning to make it to the Hill O'Many Stanes tonight, it's a beautiful spot. Care to join us?'

'No thanks. We've just come from there.'

The faces of both strangers fell in unison.

The first stranger glanced at my van and saw with horror that it was facing in the opposite direction to his own.

'You're not, are you?' he asked slowly. 'You're not... doing it anticlockwise?'

I nodded.

The two strangers looked at each other, astonished and not a little afraid.

'Well nice talking to you, we'd better be off. Long drive ahead.' They both jumped back into their van, the man fumbling for his keys. He fired up the engine and headed out of the lay-by.

'Good luck', the tall woman called out to me as they disappeared into the east.

I watched them fade into the early morning mist.

At that point Russell poked his head out. 'Who was that?' he asked.

'Just a couple of nutters', I told him. 'Or a couple more, anyway. Don't worry your pretty little baldy head about it. Get the tea on.'

He went back in. I strode to the edge of the cliff and looked down at the crashing surf. The rising sun was not reflected in the ocean here. We were at the north of the island. The sun travelled behind us in the southern sky. Without this light playing on the surface the grey sea looked stark, uniform and cold. I had a strange sense that it was waiting for something.

17

The next couple of days were very strange. Will was being miserable, for reasons I'll get to in a minute. Graeme just stared out of the window as we drove, lost in his own world. He made no attempt to talk to us or to tell us about his story. He seemed to think that it was our job to ask. Russell, I would guess, took the opposite view, that it was Graeme's role to ask about us. With both these men competing for the 'most inscrutable and enigmatic' badge, the van stayed eerily silent.

The silence generated an odd mood in the van. But perhaps silence is not the right word, for we always had the constant moaning of both the engine and the wind. Perhaps it was the lack of information in those sounds that disorientated us. The parts of our brains that analyse the sounds in our ears were working as normal, it's just that they kept coming up blank. If there was information in the sound-scape of those days, it spoke a language that was entirely foreign to us.

I fell into a kind of dull funk and travelled along those roads in a daze. I was aware of the power of the scenery around me, for you couldn't ignore the terrible beauty outside the windows. The weather had picked up considerably since we left England and the low Autumn sunlight made those Highlands glow. And yet, being only half alive, I remained safe from all that unnatural, inhuman beauty. Even when we stopped I rarely left the van.

The problem was the route. The road network as we knew it had pretty much broken down. Finding the nearest 'A' road to the coast was no longer an automatic process, as much of the coast was untroubled by any roads at all. What 'A' roads there were weaved in and out of the landscape in what, on the map, appeared to be a random or foolish manner. It was only when we drove the roads and saw how they fitted into the landscape that their placement justified itself. As a result we often found ourselves undertaking epic, twisty detours which eventually returned us to our path just a few miles further along the way. We drove, but we didn't get anywhere. We went up, and we went down. We rolled and turned and looped and rolled again. The landscape toyed with us. The sun appeared to dance around the sky, hopping around as if teasing us. That was an illusion, of course. The sun would have been as steady as always, circling round and round on its journey to nowhere, achieving nothing except claiming this planet as its own. It was we that were rolling around like flotsam.

The noisy silence seemed to be affecting us all differently. I switched off, but Russell seemed to come more alive. It was silence that he was seeking, after all, with the stupid music-fast that he was inflicting on the rest of us. I noticed that the little darting motions he often made with his head and eyes were more constant than usual. I saw that the little dances his fingers made whenever a new thought struck him kept coming, regular and undisguised. I don't know what he was hoping to get out of his period without music, but it struck me for the first time that he might actually find it.

And Will? Will was being miserable, sullen and uncommunicative. He was not being uncommunicative in the same way I was, which I like to think had a winsome, dreamy air about it. He was more of your standard miserable bastard, tutting and wincing and scowling. Fortunately though I was barely present, so I didn't allow myself to get annoyed by this. Russell, as usual, simply didn't notice. He was too busy being Russell.

Will's foul mood began on the morning of the twelfth day. We were parked up overlooking the Isle of Ewe, surrounded still by the never-ending wilderness. Will had risen early and, as he always does now, headed down to the shore to hunt for his precious bottles. I left him to it, as was my custom. But I watched from the headland as he scurried up to the surf. He was tiny from this vantage point, yet I could see him well enough to watch as he checked the rock pools and scoured the beach. The sea was a brown colour, full of sand and silt. It seemed agitated.

Russell joined me, while Graeme slept late. It seemed as good a time as any to talk to him about his problem with music.

I didn't expect any insight, of course. There's no point in asking Russell why he does anything. He has no idea. He lives in a bubble of constant surprise, always amazed by the events of the previous couple of minutes. Still, there's no harm in trying to talk to him as if he was a properly functioning human, for politeness' sake if nothing else.

'So, explain to me your problem with music,' I asked, as bluntly as I could.

He screwed up his face.

'I was a musician, like you, and I gave up music, also like you. But it wasn't enough. It won't let me be.'

'What won't? Music?'

He nodded. 'It's like a drug.'

'It can make you dress stupid and hang around with idiots, so I suppose you could say it's like a drug.'

'Actually scratch that, it's not like a drug. It *is* a drug. It's something that you take to change how you're feeling. It's a mood changer, it's uppers or downers. It triggers emotions that you shouldn't really be experiencing at that point. It's fake, ultimately, fake emotions. Or at the very least, emotions that someone else is having for you. Too much of it does you no good at all.'

I thought about this. 'As drugs go, it's a pretty healthy one, isn't it?'

He shook his head. 'It should be, but it's all wrong, isn't it? The balance has gone.' He looked me in the face to see if I understood. I didn't.

'The balance of what?' I asked.

He waved his arms as if trying to express something beyond words.

'All of it. Our culture. We're not being pushed anymore. We're being jostled.'

'What, by music?'

'By everything. But music is the best barometer. It's our canary in the coal mine. It tells us when we're choking on the psychic pollution.'

I wasn't really getting him.

'We used to be able to listen, didn't we?' he continued. 'There used to be normal life, dull as hell but solid and real. You can read about it in history books. And occasionally you could leave it with music. Music allowed you to escape to another place. Maybe an hour or so every few days, but those little trips to the other place were enough. It was healthy. It was good.

'But it grew, and grew. All music, all media, it got everywhere. And with quantity came competition and with competition it got more demanding. It started shouting to be noticed, demanding our attention. 'Have you seen this? Have you heard this? But you must! You must!'

'It reached the stage where it had us. It had consumed us. We can't escape from it now. We live there, in the other place. But we try to get back to the dull and solid world because we fear it needs us. So we stop listening. We tune it all out. We couldn't become absorbed in it in any case, what with all the shouting and the hysteria and the pretend jeopardy. And that leaves us nowhere. We're not absorbed in the other place, and we're not in the solid. We're in limbo. We can't concentrate. We can't listen.'

'I mean, can you even remember what it was like to be bored? I can't. I'd love to be bored. Imagine it, imagine not having all those demands on you. Imagine that.'

He fell into a low mumble at this point and I could no longer follow him. He suddenly looked much older than I have ever seen him.

'So - you want to be bored, is that it? You want to be bored in the real world?' I asked.

He turned and studied me, seemingly hurt that I had not understood.

'No Pen', he replied. 'I want to be able to listen again.'

I turned and looked down at Will on the shore. He bent down and pulled a bottle from the water. Even from this distance, I could see that this bottle was not blue like all the others. It was red. And it was clear from his body language that this had surprised him too.

I watched as, hesitantly, he drew a slip of paper out of the bottle. He tucked the red bottle under his arm as he unfurled the paper and read what he had to say. He seemed to spend a long time looking at that tiny square of paper and when he had finished he looked up and his shoulders slumped. Then he looked down at the paper and bottle, as if trying to decide what to do. Soon, he made his decision. He threw the bottle down, smashing it on the rocks. He tore up the paper and hurled the bits into the waves. Then he marched back across the bay and returned to the van.

I asked him if everything was all right. He nodded but said very little, and indeed continued to say very little for some time.

18

Glasgow!

Have you ever arrived in Glasgow from the north? It's like sighting land after months at sea. Man-made objects! People doing stuff! Pavements! Litter! Consumer options!

Life on a human scale!

I tell you, your opinion of Glasgow is very different if you approach it from the north rather than the east or south. We wandered the streets in a daze, as if we were unable to really believe that such a place could really exist. I went into shops and bought things. I couldn't even tell you what they were, it only mattered that they were things.

We were sat in a small Italian restaurant near the Tolbooth Steeple in Merchant City. This was the place that Graeme had promised to buy us a meal at when we met him four days ago, on the north-east coast.

'Well?' he asked. 'Do you know why I brought you here?'

Me, Will and Russell looked around. We were sat near the window at a cramped little wicker table. There didn't seem to be anything distinctive about the place. It wasn't even that nice, if I'm being honest. The menu had photographs of food on it. That's never a good sign.

'You'll have to tell us,' said Will.

Graeme gestured to the room around him. 'This used to be the Zodiac!'

Graeme had expected us to look delighted. Instead, we sat there awkwardly, not looking at each other. The Zodiac was the club where we played our last ever gig together. It was the place where our band died.

Our last ever gig was not a happy time. It was only a few months after I had caught Russell in bed with a groupie, for one thing. We were still adjusting to the new status of our relationship when we played that last gig. We had become 'work colleagues', a distinct shift from our previous relationship status as 'everything'.

'Don't you remember? This used to be the bar, and the stage was up those stairs over there,' he explained.

'I'd forgotten all about that place,' muttered Will, with his attention focused on his meatballs in spaghetti.

'How long ago did it close?' I asked Graeme.

'No idea. It's been gone a long time and this area has changed a heap since then. It's all 'up and coming' around here. I doubt you'd find anyone around here that can remember the old place.'

He turned and pointed towards a door half-hidden by the bar.

'And remember down there? That was where they had the dressing room, remember that? Big and dry, but miles from the stage. And you three just sat in there and whined at each other about some shit song title or other.'

'It was a shit album title,' I corrected him. Graeme was pushing the conversation towards the awkward zone, the no-go area that we'd avoided during the rest of the journey. Should we go there now? It was a good a time as any. If scabs are not meant to be picked, then why are they so eminently pick-able?

I knew that this shit album title wasn't really the reason the band ended, of course. The crack we carried was deep and long-growing. That argument was only the surface of the problem, the portal through which all the subconscious warfare seeped out. Taken out of context it seems like the trivial issue it really is. But loaded with the baggage of the past, even mentioning it seemed charged.

The argument was about whether or not 'The Colour of the Sea' was a shit name for an album.

And I think we can all agree that 'The Colour of the Sea' is a shit name for an album, and that the real issue is why on earth Russell would not only fail to see that, but demand that we use it.

'It may have been a shit title,' said Russell, a little huffy, 'but I was certain that it was the right title.'

'Even though,' Will prompted him, 'both myself and Penny vetoed it.'

Will was being kind here. I'm not sure he did veto it. As I remember events, the argument was between myself and Russell while Will did his best to calm us down and mediate. It's not my place to speak for him of course, but I feel he believed that the shitness of the album title was of less importance than the death of the band.

'But you said so yourself,' Russell replied, 'all our album titles were shit. Our song titles were shit. Our band name was shit. One more shit title shouldn't have been a big deal.'

'But it was shit on a different level', I interrupted. 'It was pretentious shit. Most of our titles were meaningless on a stupid level. That's fine. But this was meaningless on a wanky level. What was it trying to say? The colour of the sea, yeah okay, the sea's a nice colour. Is that your point? Is there anything else that that title is trying to say there?'

Russ shook his head. 'Not that I'm aware of,' he said.

'But it sounds like it might mean something, and that's what's wrong with it. It had the illusion of some depth. And if that title appealed to anyone, if they bought the record because it was called 'The Colour of the Sea', then they'd be witless fucks. And then we'd be one of those bands that witless fucks listen to.'

I could feel myself getting angry again. It was like there was a deep well of trouble underneath that stupid title, and it was as turbulent now as it was originally. I didn't understand why this was. How could something so trivial be so potent?

'If it helps,' Russ said, calmly trying to talk me down, 'I agree with you. You were dead right then and you are dead right now. All I can say is, despite all that, I just couldn't shake the conviction that it was the title we needed. I don't know why that is. You know how sometimes you are just hit with a notion? I know it's pretentious-sounding, I know it's meaningless. Or at least, if there is any meaning there, I don't know what it is.'

I looked at him.

'Russell, there definitely is no meaning there', I told him.

He shrugged.

'Yeah, like that's my fault!' he replied.

'Ah, quit your bickering!' said Graeme suddenly. We all turned and looked at him in surprise.

'Honestly. If you would just be honest with each other! Look, I'm not on your path. I'm on my own path. Technically I'm the outsider here and with my perspective I can see what you three cannot. You think you're all separate, don't you? You think that because you haven't seen each other for fifteen years or whatever, that your paths are all separate? I'll tell you this for nothing. You're stuck with each other. You're entwined. You're all wrapped up into a single thread. And that's good, you know? That's as good as it gets, to be tangled up with others. Did you not find it strange that you three could all make this trip? That none of you had children or partners or responsibilities? At your age? You're more than the sum of your parts, you three. And it doesn't matter a jot whether you can see that or not, or whether you all head off and never see each other ever again. But I'm mentioning it now, because I thought you'd like to know.'

He stood up. 'Now, if you'll excuse me, I have my own bullshit to attend to. So thank you for the lift. Good luck on your pointless journey. And make the most of it, okay?'

He gave a little half-wave, turned, and left the restaurant. We sat in silence and watched him go.

'He's gone and left us the bill, hasn't he?' said Russell.

Me and Will nodded.

19

It was the 16th day. The land was reassuringly flat and the road was long and straight. Will was driving. We were on the A747 between Stranraer and Carlisle. Outside the sky was blue and, protected as we were from the chill of the Irish Sea, the landscape looked unseasonably Spring-like. It helped that the van had had its first wash since we began, and the windows were now allowing sunlight in once more. It danced around the cabin.

Russell missed all this. He was sleeping in the back.

I looked at Will as he drove. He was concentrating on the narrow strip of road between the fields and the rocky shore. This would be good time to get him to talk about himself, I thought. I knew well enough that there are only two times that men are able to talk openly about themselves: after 2am in the morning, and when they are driving at speeds greater than 40mph.

The arrival of a row of neat white bungalows on the left-hand side of the road indicated that we had reached Fort William. On the right hand side was a small stretch of dark rocks and the flat sea beyond. It was the best excuse I had for breaking the silence.

'I never realised before how many houses seem to exist solely to look out to sea', I said. 'Especially bungalows. They're like the Moai statues of Easter

Island. They line up in neat little rows on the edge of cliffs and just stare at it. What's so important about staring at the sea? Will it cease to exist if we take our eyes off it?'

'Perhaps they're not looking at the sea. Perhaps they're avoiding looking at the land behind them,' he said.

'Perhaps you're a miserable arse.'

'I am no such thing. I am a stable and moderately content arse.'

'Well maybe. But I am worried about you.'

He smiled. Almost.

'That's very kind Penny. But I don't need worrying about.'

'It's dangerous to have such a big hole in your life', I told him. 'Holes don't stay open forever and something will come along to fill it. The trouble is, with a hole as big as yours, it could be something overwhelming. And not necessary something positive.'

As I spoke I very deliberately looked at the blue bottle on the dashboard, knowing that he was aware enough to pick up on my meaning.

He dropped down a gear and slowed the van as we reached a small roundabout by the harbour. I then had to wait for him to drive out the other side of town before he would reply because, as I mentioned earlier, men can only talk about themselves in the day when they are travelling at 40mph or more.

'You're assuming that there's a big hole in my life because Celine died and yeah, on a practical level that's true. But on another level, things are not that different. I still talk to her. I still find out what she thinks.'

I smiled. 'That is lovely. I understand what you mean. My grandfather was the same. He said he still had my Nan to keep him company after she died.'

'I'm pretty sure you don't understand, you know. From the tone of your voice, I mean, you sound all sentimental and American. I'm not talking about platitudes. I'm not being insincere. I'm talking about a real thing.'

'I know', I said calmly.

'No you don't. You're thinking, 'Oh her spirit visits him' or 'Death can't separate true soul-mates', that sort of crap. It's not that. I hate all that. It's why we can't talk about these things. I'm not being wishy-washy or spiritual, or whatever. I'm being a hard-nosed materialist. Look, what are we? What is it that makes us who we are, or what we think and how we behave? We're a pattern of connections between neurons. That's us, that's our personalities, our memories, our prejudices. That's our sense of humour, our emotions, our sense of self. We're neuron patterns. The map of which brain cells are connected through which synapses. That's pretty unarguable, isn't it?'

I nodded.

'But big chunks of our brain are not there to create us. They're there to model the world outside us. When you meet someone, neurons connect and form a memory of them. If you meet them briefly then it's just a quick sketch done in broad strokes. The more you know someone, the more that sketch is improved. Details are added. You learn their history, their tastes, how they react, how they smell. Endless details, using more and more neurons and more and more synapses. And for every new thing you learn, your model of them becomes more complicated, more detailed.'

'But what is that person you're getting to know? That person is a pattern of neuron connections. And what are you doing? You're making a model of their pattern of neuron connections with your pattern of neuron connections. And okay, it's not identical, but if you're with that person for decades - I mean really with them, you're absorbed by them - it gets pretty good. It's not the same but it's... functionally equivalent, I guess. It can predict how they will react. It knows what films they will like, or what they want for lunch and when they will get annoyed.'

'And there seems to be a point, a tipping point, when the model in your brain gets sufficiently detailed and it suddenly works by itself. The model becomes self-sufficient. It becomes alive. Humans are considered to be conscious in a way that animals aren't because our patterns of neuron connections have become so complicated that we've become aware. This is just the same thing. A sufficiently complicated pattern of neurons becomes a living, conscious thing. And the model of Celine in my head is sufficiently advanced that it works just like the pattern of neurons in her head that made her who she was. It's not 100% accurate, but it's good enough. My head is, basically, a backup. She's downloaded herself into me. And when I talk to her she can surprise me and make me laugh in exactly the same way she used to.'

'And you might say that that's not really the same. But ask yourself, who was it that you knew in life, in all that time you spent together? Was it the original? Or did you only know the model you built of them? If you think back to when you got to know them and how your perception of them changed as your model grew, then you have to wonder if it was really that model that you knew, that you spent your life with. We can only know people through the models we build of them.'

'And so when your Granddad says that your Nan is keeping him company, he's not in denial, he's not a daft old sod. It's that your Nan is keeping him company. A very good copy of your Nan, and the only one he ever knew. The same one that he spent his life with. And I'm not saying that it works for everyone. Not everyone creates a model complicated enough to 'live'. Maybe not everyone can. You hear a lot of old people talk about this so maybe it normally takes a lifetime. Maybe

I've been very lucky to get her modelled in fifteen years or so. I don't know.

I was quiet. It was a lot to take in. He glanced at me.

'Well you did ask', he said.

'What do you mean, 'the model gets so complicated that it comes alive?" I asked. 'How do you mean, 'alive'?'

He took a deep breath.

'Christ, how to explain that? It's pretty obvious in practice. I mean, you hear about all these people who are schizophrenic or who have multiple personality disorders, or who talk to spirit guides or whatever. Their brains have spawned autonomous neuron patterns that feel separate to their owner. No, hang on, I've got a better example than those. Okay, think of it this way. You've got all these people saying there's no such thing as God. And you've got all these people saying that they know full well that there is a God because they themselves personally know God, not as an abstract idea but as a self-apparent presence in their lives. Now, this is the same thing. The believers have usually been brought up in religious environments where they spent much of their youth studying God, thinking about God, talking about God. And all the time they are building up the pattern of neurons which holds the idea of God. And if that model gets detailed enough, then it pops into life and becomes a living thing. For them, anyway. And that divide, between wondering whether God exists and knowing God personally, it's a pretty self-evident divide. We all know which side of it we fall. Just as we all know if our partner is gone, or if we can still hear them.

I groped about for some words to make sense of what I was thinking.

'So are you saying, that God is real? Or not real?'

Will screwed up his face.

'That's none of my concern, if I'm honest. I've gone off on a bit of a tangent. This wasn't what I wanted to talk about. But as you ask, God is real for some but not real for others.'

'But that 'real for some', that's not really real, is it?'

'For those people, God is as real as anyone else they know, or any other pattern of neurons. I wouldn't get too hung up on the word 'real', if I were you. Their God is as real as they are. Or think of it this way. Their God is an autonomous neuron pattern. But you yourself, what makes you you, are also an autonomous neuron pattern. You said so at the start. Following that logic, if their God isn't real, then how real are you?'

I looked at him with fresh eyes.

'I'm not sure I ever really appreciated this before', I said, 'but you're a weird fucker.'

He nodded.

'Celine has wondered how long it would take you to pick up on that', he said.

20

Of all the places to find a quiet pub, we finally found one in Blackpool. Perhaps there is a greater need for bars with no music in the back streets of loud, brash towns.

The pub was brown and shadowy, despite the low afternoon sun streaming through the window. Russell was delighted with the place however, for he had not been able to enter a pub since Whitby. He sat on the cracked leather bench and played with a beer mat as he studied his Guinness and crisps.

He was sitting there alone. Will had made his excuses and left for a walk shortly after we arrived. The implication was that he was kindly giving me and Russell some time together. That may be what he had convinced himself of, but it's pretty clear that he just prefers wandering off alone.

Well, I say 'alone'...

I had also left Russell, if only to go and sit on the toilet and let time slip past. Despite Will's best intentions, I was not too eager to spend time alone with Russell. It felt a little unnatural. We'd nothing in common, but we felt that we should have. The toilet was a good excuse to sit and think of a way to ditch him for the afternoon. It was an excuse to fuck off by myself for a while.

I think all three of us needed some time alone, if I'm honest.

Slowly, I became aware that something was wrong.

It took me an age to recognise exactly what it was. I looked up, and around the cubicle. Was it the air? Was there something wrong with the air?

Then I noticed the regular twitching motion of my foot, and it hit me that I was listening to music.

My music, to be exact.

Which didn't seem possible. I strained to place exactly what I was hearing. It clicked into place the moment the second guitar kicked in. This was the third song on the second side of the one solo album I made after I left the band.

This was the Penny Fuckhammer album.

It was an album that was released over fifteen years ago, and which nobody bought. It was the album that ended my musical career.

It was bloody good though.

I kept listening.

It was really good.

But was I really hearing it, or was it somehow playing in my head? The sound had a strange unreal quality, but then bathroom acoustics are always odd. I pulled up my knickers and stuck my head out the cubicle.

It was louder there, and there was a speaker on the wall, above the door.

I moved my head from side to side. The music was definitely outside of me. That was, however, the stranger of the two scenarios. What was going on?

And listen to my voice! Wow, I couldn't sing like that now. I couldn't sing like that then, to be honest. Something just clicked on those few days in the studio and it just poured out of me.

Of course, if the pub was playing this utterly obscure track in the ladies toilet, there seemed a good chance that they would be playing it to the rest of the pub. Where Russell was sitting.

'Well', I thought. 'This is going to be interesting'.

I ran through his possible reactions in my head. He may have stood up and walked out the moment it came on, without recognising what it was. This seemed the least troublesome scenario, so I crossed my fingers for it. The other alternatives, I knew, would be more emotionally complicated and Russell was never good with emotionally complicated.

I quietly stepped out of the ladies and into the main bar. Wow, it sounded great in there.

I looked across at Russell. He didn't see me. His eyes were closed. His head was back slightly, swaying with the bass notes as his right foot and left thumb kept time. He may have been mumbling a few words under his breath, but I couldn't be sure.

He was utterly lost inside the music.

This was awkward.

The thing to do was to leave quietly. I tiptoed over to the bar in order to retrieve the spade that I had left leaning there. At the bar I noticed the laptop on the shelf behind, which was the source of this music. A blue bar highlighted the line that displayed the track number, title, album and artist:

'7. Slim Hipped Gambler. Penny Fuckhammer. Penny Fuckhammer.'

Then I noticed that the playlist was titled 'All-time favourites' and something lovely just melted all over me. I took my hand off the spade handle and, I'm slightly embarrassed to admit, I let out a gentle little whimper.

I went back to the table and silently I sat down next to Russell. I put my hand on his gently, without disturbing him.

I closed my eyes and listened to the music with him. I listened to that music for the first time in years. If I'm honest, I listened to that music for the first time ever.

21

We spent the night in Liverpool, staying with some friends of Will's. Their names were Mark and Clare, and they lived what seemed a tolerable suburban existence in a tree-lined street in Huyton. That's pretty much all I could tell you about them, though, because their conversation kept well away from anything personal. I could see why Will liked them so much.

I had hoped a night with Will's friends would fill in a few gaps. I didn't know Celine well, for example. Will had met her near the very end of the band, when I had been too overwhelmed with my own crap to pay her much attention. I wasn't entirely sure about how she died. Mark and Clare had known them both well throughout their marriage, so you would think they would talk about her, wouldn't you? That seems reasonable, does it not?

Apparently not.

Let me tell you something. In December I am moving to Iceland. My brother's ex-wife runs a coffee shop in Reykjavik and she has asked me to move out there and co-manage it with her. How about that? I'm excited, as you can imagine. I have never lived abroad before. When a new path appears and you can't see where it is going, that is always exciting. I don't yet know where I will live, or how long I will stay out there. I feel like I've come to the edge of a map, and the only way to see what lies ahead is to go forward. You can understand why I wanted to mention it, can't you? It's a big deal for me.

But can I tell Will and Russell about it? It appears not. There are very few polite ways to move the conversation onto your own future when that subject holds no interest to those you are with. I could just blurt it out, I guess, but that doesn't do it justice. So it remains one of the unshared events that surround us, one of those many things that exist for individuals but not for groups.

But all that was last night. Now, all eyes were on the road. We were waiting to drive over a little reminder of our history. Following an early start (and a drive up and down the Wirral, because that's the rules) we had entered North Wales. Our focus was then on bilingual road markings. Soon we would see the word 'SLOW' painted on the road ahead of a junction, followed by 'ARAF', its Welsh equivalent. 'SLOW ARAF' the road will say, as if it was promoting the name of our band, The Slow Arafs.

If I had any advice for aspiring musicians it would be not to pick a band name that includes the word 'slow'. If I could do it all over again, I'd keep clear of uninspiring words altogether. You don't get to be anyone's favourite band by calling yourself 'slow'.

But it was Russell's band, Russell's name and this was Russell's territory. He had grown up around here, the unfashionable end of North Wales, and he'd spent his formative days dreaming of leaving. This is where he shut himself away in his room with his guitar, content to spend his days practising in isolation. This is where he taught himself to write songs, and sing, and where he dreamt up the band that he would front. As I understand it, the band had that name about five years before it had any members. Russell believed that these road markings would be constant promotion for the band. He hadn't realised that the legend 'SLOW ARAF' was a regional quirk, that most of the country just used 'SLOW' and other parts of Wales went for 'ARAF SLOW'.

There wasn't any evidence that the parts of Wales that had 'SLOW ARAF' road markings were any more interested in our records, either, so the whole scheme was an abject failure on just about every level.

But when we saw our first 'SLOW ARAF' road markings, I felt a sudden surge of excitement. This reaction took me by surprise. I hadn't realised I was capable of... what was it? Nostalgia? Something unnecessary, anyway. The three of us gave a spontaneous cheer when those words scrolled into view, a cheer that peaked as we passed over them.

I watched the other cars, blindly and routinely driving over that name as they must do thousands and thousands of times every day. None of them gave a little cheer. I doubt many of them even consciously noticed, so blind are we to extraneous information when we're driving. I wondered if anyone else saw those words and remembered an also-ran guitar band from over a decade and a half earlier? I knew then that no-one did.

Most chunks of history get lost eventually, of course, but I don't understand the priorities of that process. Moments that seem important at the time are usually the first to blow away, as irrelevant and inconsequential as last year's *X Factor* final. Our band was just one of them. It was gone now, and no-one had any reason to think of it again.

Then there are moments that seem trivial at the time but which gain stature as they recede away. Their pull grows stronger the further away from them we are, as if we were linked to them by a bungee cord. You could spend a lifetime trying to understand why our psyches snag onto those moments above all others.

A wave of sadness hit me then. It took me a moment to recognise what it was, because it was so unexpected. Why should I care that the only people who cheer in shared nostalgia as they drive over road markings are me, Russell and Will? That is how it should be, after all.

It is the duty of the past to fuck off and leave the present alone.

There was nothing to do but wait for those feelings to pass. We drove deeper into Wales.

22

I was on a stone boat. Let me explain that. I was on part of a stone quay which was built to look like a boat, with masts and a cabin. I didn't really understand what was going on, if I'm honest.

'What is this Will?'

'It's a stone boat.'

Some things deny explanation. You just have to go with them and accept that someone must once have been really into the idea. Will had just found another blue bottle in the sea, and hence was too happy to connect with my level of bemused confusion.

We were in Portmeirion, a fake Italianate village built into the woodland near Porthmadog. It is a jumble of columns, statues, domes and towers that cling to the hillside and overlook a wide coastal inlet. It's not real, basically, in the same way that Disneyland isn't real. It's a fake village for you to walk around and marvel at. But there is a point to Disneyland. It is designed to make money. It is designed to further brand synergy and to exploit related markets, and all that sort of stuff - you know the deal. But Portmeirion? It only exists to be beautiful. Imagine that.

It'll never catch on.

The area around Snowdonia and Anglesea is the most unfathomable part of the country. It is a place apart. There are certain shades of dark green there that don't exist anywhere else. Portmeirion should have been wildly out of place, were it not for that fact that this was a landscape where anything could happen.

Portmeirion was called the 'Xanadu of Wales' when it was built in the early 20th Century. It was the playground of Noel Coward, George Bernard Shaw and Bertrand Russell. I mentioned this to Will.

'Do you know what Bertrand Russell said about music?' Will asked. 'Or he may have got it off George Bernard Shaw, but one of them. He said it was 'the brandy of the damned.' There's an image for you, the brandy of the damned. I'm not sure what I think about that. I'm both delighted and appalled by it.'

I shrugged. 'Don't worry about it. The 'damned' bit is just Bertrand Russell's baggage. It's a very deterministic word. He knew for a fact that we would all be wiped out by a nuclear holocaust by the mid-1980s, remember? 'The brandy of the damned' is him being pretty cheery, in that context. And to put that in perspective, Bertrand Russell was wildly believed to be a genius, one of the greatest British thinkers of the century. He was the most humane and clear-sighted intellectual that we had. So when he logically deduced mid-80s global genocide that was a serious downer, because it was an absolute certainty. Calling something 'damned' is to claim knowledge of the future, because that's the whole point of being damned, that there's no hope for you. Of course, you can count the amount of people who really do have knowledge of the future on the fingers of no hands.'

I had lost my respect for rationality long ago. The intellect is not the tool for discerning the future, it never has been and it never will be. It ranks somewhere behind random guessing and answering every question with the statement 'It'll be fine.' Personally I try to rely on gut instinct. I knew then, for example, that after Russell had finished talking to the two women he was with he would join us on the stone boat, clap his hands in front of his chest, and hold them together whilst he smiled at first Will and then me. I don't know how I knew that, as I keep the intellect well away from my gut. But I knew it.

The two women Russell was talking to were fans. He had been recognised for the first time on our journey. The two women were giddy with excitement and couldn't take their eyes off him. I could hear them singing snatches of his shit number one single back at him, then giggling nervously. I confess this did make me smirk. I was also amused by their age, because they seemed too old to be giggling at a pop star. But then I remembered that I was probably a good five years older than they were.

Russell gave them both a little peck on the cheek and walked over to us. He joined us on the stone boat, clapped his hands in front of his chest, and held them together while he smiled at first Will and then me. 'This place is amazing!' he said.

We looked out to sea while Will and Russell talked about *The Prisoner. The Prisoner* was a TV series from the 1960s that was filmed there, and which they felt I had a duty to know about. You can't be in Portmeirion for long without hearing about this strange psychedelic TV show. It's one of the things that makes this place such an odd mix of influences. Portmeirion is a mishmash of holiday location, destination restaurant, pottery market and cult TV landmark. Anything, in other words, which comes along and which might contribute to its upkeep. Having been built with the sole goal of beauty, anything they stumble upon that might pay the bills is embraced. It is not an easy job to justify Portmeirion's place in the world.

Will explained that in *The Prisoner,* Patrick McGoohan played a kidnapped spy who was unable to escape from this village. It seemed daft to me. This was no prison camp, and there seemed little to keep him here. The village was surrounded by thick forest, but it had a huge expanse of beach in front of it. I pointed out across the inlet, to the mountains beyond.

'Couldn't he swim? He could have swum right across there if the tide was right.'

Will shook his head.

'If he tried that a big white bubble thing would have emerged out of the water and caught him.'

Bubble thing? My mind had wandered a little and I wasn't sure that I had heard him correctly. It sounded like he said a bubble thing would catch him if he swam away, which didn't sound plausible. I tried to work out if I was the butt of some strange joke, the point of which I was completely missing.

'That doesn't seem very likely,' I said.

'It doesn't matter if it's likely or not,' said Will. 'Why shouldn't big white bubbles come out of the sea? Who knows what's down there? Anything can emerge from the depths.'

I looked out to sea again.

'What the fuck are you on about, Will?'

He paused for a second. 'I'm talking about a TV programme, you know? Fiction and the imagination. I'm not talking about the real sea.'

I nodded. Even with that cleared up, the image of giant white balls emerging from the sea still seemed troubling. For some reason I couldn't quite disconnect the concept of the sea and the concept of the imagination, the mental world. At some point those two ideas must have merged within me somehow, although I couldn't think when or how.

I shook my head and made an effort to wrench them apart. I assumed that this was the sensible thing to do, but what did I know? I was the one standing on a stone boat, after all.

23

That night Russell slept in the tent with Will while I had the back of the van. I slept fitfully for a while, then jerked awake. I instantly knew I had no hope of going back to sleep.

I was unusually awake, more awake then during the day. I felt like my eyes were the size of golf balls and I could see every crack and bubble in the paint on the ceiling of the van. I could tell from the silence that dawn was many hours away, yet it was unusually bright. I felt compelled to leave the van. I knew I had to do something physical if I was to become tired enough to sleep again. Moving quietly in order to not wake the boys, I opened the side door of the van and swung my bare feet out and onto the grass. It did not feel damp, or cold.

Outside, even the ocean seemed quiet. I knew something was wrong but I could not say what. Slowly I scanned the moonlit Welsh field; the tent, the van and all else was still. They seemed fragile, as if they would shatter if I moved quickly. Not even the wind was moving tonight.

I looked out to sea. The moonlight flickered across its surface in chaotic little flashes. I glanced up at the moon, which hung full and round above the waves.

This seemed odd, for I hadn't expected it to be full. Surely it wasn't time for the next full moon yet?

'How long have we been driving for?' I thought. Was I losing track of time?

At that moment the clouds to the left of the moon scattered. They revealed a second moon. It was an identical size and slightly redder in colour.

There were two moons in the sky.

The shock wiped all thought from my mind. I stood numbly in front of it, frozen like a garden gnome in a warzone.

Then my mind ricocheted back into my skull, and my jaw dropped, and the heavens flooded in through my eyes and my brain turned to mush.

My heart pounded. My breathing became fast and shallow. Terror tensed every muscle in my body. Unable to move, I waited in horror of what would happen next. The world I knew and understood had shattered and dissolved in a fraction of a second, and I had no way of knowing what would follow. But time passed, and nothing changed. No new shocks erupted and my heart kept beating. My fear remained, but there was no danger. There were just two bright moons in the sky, like a Gothic Tattooine, and I stared up at both of them.

After an age, I thought I'd better tell someone.

I dashed over to the tent and unzipped the entrance. Leaning in, I grabbed Russell's leg and shook it hard.

A fraction of a second before his eyes opened the moonlight behind me dimmed. I knew instinctively what had just happened. I stopped shaking Russell immediately but it was too late. He was awake and was calling me names.

'Fuck off! Fuck off you crazy bitch!' were his exact words.

I turned around and looked up at the sole moon in the sky. That pale half-moon shone down at me. I turned back to Russell, unsure what to say.

'What you doing, Pen?'

'Sorry Russell, you were snoring like a bastard. It was doing my head in'.

He glowered at me, shut his eyes and returned to sleep.

I re-zipped the tent as quietly as I could. I then scanned the sky for ten minutes or so, until I convinced myself that it was normal, and routine. Then I went and squatted around by the far side of the van, by the front wheel arch, away from the moon. I sat there for a couple of hours smoking cigarettes and cursing this stupid journey. This is the problem with doing weird things. If you behave like a reasonable person, then the world will be reasonable back. If you step outside of the norm, however, and act in freaky ways, then the world will match you step for step.

I fell asleep.

When I woke I was cold and damp from the dew. My neck ached. Dawn had risen but no-one else was close to waking. 'Christ', I thought, 'what a weird dream.' But I knew that it wasn't a dream. So I stood up, let the blood return to my legs, took some deep breaths and told myself never to think about it again.

24

We were in Pembrokeshire. The original plan had been to stop somewhere around St. David's but that afternoon's drive, especially the coast road south of Aberysthwyth, had been so blissfully beautiful that we kept driving as the sun slowly fell towards the Irish Sea. The sun was in no hurry and neither were we. The air subtly turned golden and I felt that I was being handed a gift of some type.

We were on the road north of Newgale. The road had kept a few fields between us and the cliffs since leaving St. David's, and it was about to sweep down a hill and take us down to the beach. Russell remarked that he remembered staying at a YMCA somewhere around here as a boy, when a small old man appeared from out of nowhere, stepped in front of the van and smiled.

Will managed to bring the van to a halt just in time. The man chuckled, and waved at us to step outside the van.

Strangely, we did. I walked up to him and just waited. He was short, about 5' 3", with thick silver hair and a neatly trimmed white beard. His eyes were pure blue and appeared to be far too young for his ancient face.

'Hello!' he said. 'I'm Orlando Monk!'

'Hello,' I replied.

Russell nodded at him.

'You should have a look down that lane down there', he said, pointing to a small track on our right that seemed to lead towards the cliffs. There's been an accident.'

'Oh dear,' I said.

'Nice meeting you. Bonne Chance,' he said, and turned and walked away.

'Are you not coming?' called Russell after him, but he just turned, gave a little wave, and continued on his way.

'Well', said Will to Russell, 'We'd better have a look'.

What I feel I must stress is that none of this seemed strange at the time.

The three of us walked down the lane. It was reasonably wide, and the ground was dry and firm. There were berries on the hedgerow either side, and I remember thinking that they seemed to be out of season.

The hedgerows ended and we passed across the final field before the cliffs. It's difficult to explain exactly what happened during the last part of the walk. It felt like we were walking into something monumental. Its presence increased the closer we got, like the sound from a band at a festival you're heading towards. It felt like we were on autopilot, somehow.

We had become removed from the scene, in order to cushion us from the sight that we were about to find.

We reached the end and looked down.

About 10 metres beneath us was the remains of a red van. I immediately knew that it was the same van that I had seen on the north coast of Scotland. It was also clear that the van had driven along the path we had taken, failed to stop, and fallen nose first down to the rocks and surf below. The rear of the van stuck ungainly up into the air. I tried to see in the visible passenger window to see if there was any sign of the occupants. I thought that I could see an arm.

'I think they're dead,' said Will to Russell.

I nodded. We were all so calm. We weren't quite there.

'We should go down and check,' said Will. I looked at the cliff face. It seemed possible, but unwise.

'I'll go, I'm a good climber. You two stay up here,' he continued, and we watched as he slowly and cautiously made his way down the damp cliff face. After a couple of minutes of careful climbing he reached the van. He turned back to look up at us and waved to indicate all was well. Then he dropped down onto a rock by the passenger's door and, being cautious of the shattered glass, he peered in.

'There's nothing we can do here', he called up, 'they're both dead.'

'How dead?' asked Russell.

'What do you mean, 'how dead?'' Will replied. 'You're either dead or you're not.'

'I mean, are they 'sleeping peacefully,' or 'mashed beyond belief'?'

Will peered in again. 'They're pretty dead,' he muttered.

Russ nodded. 'Come back up!' he called down.

'Hang on,' Will shouted back. 'I can see something.'

He reached into the shattered passenger window, past the thing that looked like an arm, and withdrew a blue bottle. He held it up to show us.

'They've got one of these bottles! I'm going to look in the back of the van!'

We waited as he struggled with the side door to the back of the vehicle. Because of the vertical position of the van he had to slide it upwards. Awkwardly, he squeezed underneath, and it dropped back down after him with a slam.

I glanced at Russell. We waited.

After a minute the rear doors swung open unexpectedly. Will was standing inside on the remains of the van's owner's possessions. He was holding up a green plastic case around the size of a picnic basket. He opened the lid.

'Look! Bottles!'

There were over a dozen bottles inside the plastic case. Most of them were red but a handful were blue.

'Be careful,' I called down.

'I'm coming back up. No - hang on!'

Will took each red bottle out of the case in turn, and flung them out of the van. They smashed on the rocks or vanished into the surf. He then shut the case on the remaining blue bottles.

'Okay, I'm good. Coming up!'

We watched as he carefully climbed up, bringing the plastic case with him. We then walked back to our van, still in a daze, as if nothing unusual had happened.

25

I remember a scene from my dream that night. Russell was dead. I think I'd killed him but, being a dream, no-one was too concerned about that. We were at his funeral, watching his coffin being lowered into his grave. Then my phone beeped. I looked, and I had a text from Russell. He had texted me from the coffin.

The text said, 'Thanks for that.'

I showed it to Will. He was surprised. 'That doesn't sound like him at all,' he said. 'Russell doesn't do sarcasm.'

Then I woke.

I could hear sirens in the distance. We were not far from the crashed van, having driven down the hill and parked alongside the beach. From here we could make out the red of the van at the bottom of the cliffs, and the flashing blue sirens of the emergency services above it. Only then did it occur to me that we should have rung the police yesterday.

I heated water on a camping stove and made cups of tea to keep out the cold. Will returned from his morning beach combing looking delighted and clutching another blue bottle. I could see that he really wanted to share his prize with someone so I asked to see it. Anything to avoid talking about the events at the end of the bay.

He removed the page, unfurled it and handed it over. It read:

Chapter 37.

1. If you apply meaning to a thing you have made, then you have art.

2. If you apply meaning to a person, then you have love.

3. If you apply meaning to the universe, then you have God.

4. There is an inexhaustible supply of meaning.

5. Meaning costs nothing.

6. So what's the problem again?

7. *The wise man says, 'But meaning comes and goes. Sometimes it is there, sometimes it is not. That's just how it is. I wish things were different but they are not.'*

8. *'Once you accept that, we can move on to the little matter of the meaning of meaning.'*

I read it through and handed it back with a polite smile. Will put it back in the green plastic case that he had taken from the crashed van, and which he was now using to store all of his bottle collection. It was his thing, really, it wasn't for me. I was only showing interest out of politeness.

26

It happened again on the 23rd night. I woke at around 3am in the morning and was again immediately alert. I don't know exactly what put me in that state. There was moonlight pouring into the van, but not an unnatural amount. The air was still, and perhaps not as cold as it should be. The sea continued its regular churning moan in the background, quiet and persistent. Still, something was clearly wrong.

I wrapped myself in Russell's coat, for it was close at hand and warmer than mine, then I slipped my boots on and stepped out of the van. I left the boys to their dreams.

We were parked on a stubbly field at the edge of the land. Rugged Cornish rocks tumbled down to the surf on three sides. To the east were the dramatic cliffs of Hell's Mouth and to the west lay the northern end of the long, sweeping sands of St Ives Bay. To the north, the Atlantic Ocean stretched to the horizon and beyond.

Ah, the north Cornish coast by moonlight. Is there anywhere else on earth that has that atmosphere?

I walked towards St Ives Bay. I chose that direction because the moon lay that way. It hung low over the horizon, only a few days away from full. Faint wisps of mists passed over its face, and its silver light picked out the foam of the oncoming waves.

I sat down on the edge of the field, giving me a view of the bay below me, and wrapped the oversize coat tightly around myself. I brushed my hair away from my face, then I waited for the second moon to appear.

I didn't have to wait long.

I saw it arrive, this time. It popped into place as if dragged from a vast distance before clicking into its rightful home. Once again the landscape lit up, becoming clear and distinct in every aspect apart from colour. The new moon was a little fuller than the original, but only just, and this time was at the same height as the original. They sat close in the sky, low above the horizon.

I sighed and felt content. The unknown is only frightening at first. I was prepared for this now. It was very beautiful.

Yet I slowly became uneasy. It felt like I was being watched. I turned back and saw the van at a distance. In this light and against the black of the sky, it was an unearthly silver. But there was no movement from it, and no indication that Will or Russell had woken.

I then glanced around the rest of the headland. I felt sure that in that light I would have been able to see if anyone was there, but I saw no-one. And yet, the feeling that I was being watched increased.

I turned back to the moons and gasped. For a split second I saw them as a pair of enormous eyes, and the sweep of the beach below took the place of a mouth. The effect was like a giant, black face looming over my tiny frame.

I caught myself. I had to laugh. So that was it! The two moons did look like a pair of bright shining eyes. No wonder I had the sensation of being watched. But then my laugh dissolved away into unease. The sense of being looked at hadn't disappeared with this revelation. If anything, it had got stronger. The two lunar eyes held me in their unblinking gaze.

And then, the bay moved.

Perhaps the waves shifted their approach to the beach, or the outgoing tide revealed two sandy promontories on either side of the eyes. But the line between the sea and the sand shifted.

It shifted into a smile.

I'm not proud of this, but what happened next is that I passed out. You're in no position to judge me, you understand? Wait until the sea smiles at you and see how you handle it.

I was woken by Will. It was early in the morning. I opened my eyes and saw a blue sky with a covering of turbulent purple clouds above me. The sea had taken on a greenish tint. There were, of course, no moons to be seen.

'Are you okay?' he asked.

It took me a moment to get myself together. I looked out at the bay below. It seemed colder than the night before, and I shivered.

'Look over there, Will,' I asked as I pointed. 'How does it look?'

He glanced out to sea.

'It's very nice,' he said politely.

I debated whether to take this any further. I was confused and I didn't like it. I am never confused. It is not my thing. But I also couldn't see how talking about what had happened would make anything better.

But then, if I had to talk to someone, it probably had to be someone as weird as Will.

'You don't see it looking at you?' I asked.

Will gave a confused laugh, not sure how to take the question. Politely he looked at the view I was pointing at.

And slowly, his face shifted. His eyes widened. The look on his face morphed into a mask of beatitude. He breathed slowly, and gratefully. He drank in the view.

Immediately I looked out to sea, but there was nothing unusual about the view. There were still no moons in the sky.

'Do you see it?' I asked. He didn't respond. I moved closer to him.

'Do you see the face?' I asked again.

He turned, slowly, to look at me.

'The face? What are you talking about? That's the sea.'

My mind cartwheeled. 'But... what were you looking at?'

He laughed when he recognised my confusion. I hadn't seen what he had seen, he realised, and he couldn't keep the delight out of his voice.

'Oh Penny,' he said kindly. 'You're really not going to like this, you know. It's going to wind you up something rotten.'

'What will?'

He turned his face back to the ocean. The look of slow beatitude returned.

'I can't tell you. You need to see it for yourself.'

'See what?'

'What it means.'

'What what means?'

He turned back to me.

'The colour of the sea,' he said, then he stood up and left me alone on the edge of the world.

27

I spent most of that day in the back of the van. I may have dozed, sporadically, but I did not really sleep. Instead I listened to the conversation of the boys as they drove, and particularly to what Will was saying. Unsurprisingly, he had very little to say. Men don't really communicate, do they? They just sit together and exchange facts. They'll agree on a topic, and then just inform each other of what they know on the subject. It's a wonder they don't bore themselves to tears.

After a milestone-ticking loop around Land's End, I finally fell asleep. When I woke, the van was still and Will and Russell where nowhere to be seen. I opened the side door and peered out.

We were in a flat, high field not far from the large car park in the centre of the Lizard headland. This was the southernmost tip of Britain. Russ sat nearby, attempting to build a campfire out of a few sorry-looking sticks and a newspaper. I asked him where Will was and he pointed down towards Lizard Point.

'Down there. He's gone for a walk.'

'How did he seem to you?'

Russell shrugged.

I set off to find him. I followed the path down to the southern tip of the headland and followed it as it wound down to an old lifeboat station and a small cove of greyish sand. I passed the occasional tourist but they were heading away, retreating from the chill and the oncoming dusk. The smell of damp, decaying seaweed came and went.

There was no sign of Will. I walked to the edge of the water. Despite the cold, I slipped out of my shoes and allowed the surf to break over my toes. Whoa! That woke me fully. The cold was like a brick being dropped onto my feet. Nevertheless, I remained still and slowly got used to the temperature. I felt the water froth around my toes as it rushed up the beach, and I felt it stealing away the sand underneath my heels as it flowed back into the sea.

When I turned back I noticed the tall, narrow entrance to a cave on the left of the cove. I guessed that was where Will was. I approached it slowly, peering in as I got closer. The walls were steep rock, damp and dark, but the floor was the same fine grey sand as the rest of the beach. It was strewn with the rubbish of the sea, the plastic bottles, seaweed and general rubbish that remained stranded there at high tide. The cave stank an unidentifiable organic stink. Nevertheless, there was Will, sitting cross-legged in the centre of the cave. He was looking out of the entrance and out to sea like a fucking Buddha or something. He didn't immediately notice me so I walked closer. I had a vague feeling that I was interrupting.

When I got closer I saw why he was so happy. Amongst the junk was not just one blue bottle, or two, but at least a couple of dozen. They must have been washed up into the cave and deposited there by the sea. Will had struck gold. He had gathered them together and they lay around him, like an audience.

He had found all the bottles that he had missed along the way.

'That's a lot of bottles,' I said, and he turned and smiled at me.

He didn't actually say anything, though. It occurred to me then that he had lost his mind. I felt uneasy.

'You okay, Will?' I asked.

'There's nothing to worry about Pen,' he replied. That didn't actually answer my question.

'What did you mean when you said you understood 'the colour of the sea'?'

He smiled in a distinctly punchable manner. 'Just go and look. You'll see.'

I backed out of the cave. It smelt and there was a madman in there.

I turned to the sea.

I looked at it. In this falling light it was blue with a greenish tint.

That colour did seem significant.

I stopped myself. The sea is many different colours. It can be blue, green, brown or grey, plus all variations in between. There was no single 'colour of the sea'.

There was something about that greenish blue, though. Something familiar.

Blue, green, brown or grey.

Where had I seen that greenish blue before? Why was it so comforting?

Why was I thinking of my father?

Oh.

Of course.

Blue, green, brown or grey.

We're looked at all the time, aren't we? Every day, every year, hundreds of pairs of eyes turn towards us. They might look at you with indifference, or interest, or confusion. But those are not the looks that we remember.

Sometimes, just sometimes, we are looked at with love. It's not often, you don't need me to tell you that. It may be no more than a handful of glances in a lifetime. But it's enough. There is no denying it, or forgetting it.

Blue, green, brown or grey.

And how do we know? We just see it. We see it in their eyes. And it is that moment of recognition that forms our memory. Those eyes. We remember those eyes. Be they blue, green, brown or grey.

The sea is the colour of eyes, in all their variations. It changes to match everyone in turn. Every shade in its repertoire matches someone somewhere, and if you wait long enough it will eventually become the colour of the eyes which have looked at you with love.

As it was at that moment. It was the colour of my father's eyes. Not the colour they are now, for they are greyer now, but the colour they used to be when I was a child. When he had finished work for the weekend and could play with me in the back yard, and he would look at me with love.

And when the ocean syncs with the colour of those eyes in your memory, it is like receiving that look from the whole world.

Oh sweet heaven. It is almost too much.

I held the gaze. I saw the sea.

Later, I walked back towards the van. I knew that if I had stayed too long the creeping darkness would rob the sea of its colour and I did not want to see that. If that wasn't going to happen, of course, I'd still be there now.

I saw the van in the distance. Russell was nursing his budding campfire. He had his back to me.

I thought of the paths we walk, and how we are always surprised when they lead to exactly where they were always going to lead.

'Colour of the Sea' indeed. He had no idea what that meant, of course. He didn't all those years ago, when he stuck to his guns and killed the band. He doesn't now. But he always knew that it was the correct title, and that it did have meaning even if it was not apparent.

All he knew was that he had to suggest it, and fight for it. God bless him, he doesn't understand any of this. He just does the inevitable and doesn't argue.

And that's all that we can do, isn't it? The inevitable?

I could hear him muttering under his breath, coaxing the fire to life.

'That's it my sweet, come on!'

Quietly I picked up the spade, which I'd left just outside the van. I adjusted to its weight in my hands.

I wonder if we would prefer to have a map? Would it be better if we were able to see exactly where our paths are going? It would be more pleasurable, I think. We would shrug off a weight of worry and anxiety. We would have no choice but to forgive ourselves.

'There you go! Now you've got it!'

Quietly I stood behind him. I raised the spade. I looked down at his head.

He was wearing a dark blue woollen beany hat. There was a design on it, a logo, and the hat had been put on carelessly so that that logo was facing me. It was a small orange starfish.

I projected all my strength into my arms and I brought the heavy metal shovel down onto his head.

PART THREE: RUSSELL

Day 24 (The Lizard) - Day 28 (Brighton)

28

She hit me so hard that I didn't feel it. I found myself on the floor and wondered how I had got there. All the sound, the noise of the wind and the waves, collapsed into a single note. It was so delicate that it could have been the sound of silence itself. What was happening?

I rolled onto my back and looked up. There was Penny. I felt a wave of relief hit me. She would look after me. Perhaps I had had a stroke? If I had had a stroke then I would be all right, because Penny would take care of me. She hefted her spade up.

She seemed to be speaking, but I couldn't make out her words. I forced myself to concentrate. Somehow I detuned the one note into its constituent parts, and her words drifted down to me.

'I'm not happy at all,' she said. 'This will bring me nothing but trouble and I could really do without it.'

Then she raised the spade above her head and brought it down to crack open my skull.

I jerked away at the last minute. The tip of the spade stabbed deeply into the clay earth, no more than an inch away from my head. Sound collapsed again, but the note was louder this time, and discordant.

I found myself moving. I was up on my feet, although sometimes my hands were on the ground as well, pushing myself along. My ego had shut down. My emotions and my morals were also gone. I was animal then, a reptile. I fled.

Away, away. That was all I knew. Away.

I panted. I groaned. I ran.

At some point I turned and looked behind and the sight of her - oh, the sight of her brought me back to myself. She was running in slow motion and her hair, her hair had never looked better. It streamed through the air, following the whirls and eddies of the wind. It seemed alive but then, what didn't? There was a grace to her face despite her efforts and anger. There was something so natural about the moment that stopped me. Who was I to run from this?

I remember thinking how awful it must be to be killed by a shaven-headed brute of a man, ugly as sin from every angle. No-one deserves that. She was raising the spade again as she got closer. She was preparing for another swing.

Where was I? I turned and looked. There was nothing there. I was at the edge of the world. Then I saw crashing waves way below me. I was at the edge of a cliff.

I had to see her again. I turned.

She was starting her swing as I focused. It was a perfect movement, I knew that immediately. Behind her the sky had become orange and peach, and the gulls were flying upwards. The note I was hearing shifted up an octave. It sounded different now, as if being sung by an unseen choir. Gently she tilted her head as she prepared for impact. An easy concentration made her face glow.

I wouldn't have missed it for the world.

It was a perfect blow to the side of my face. My head whipped round and my body followed. I was spinning as the world tilted. Penny fell away from me as the sea moved above. I knew how very lucky I was.

Then I was in the other world, and the cold crushed me. Sound ended. Time was speeding up, yet my movements were slowing down. I had left the coastline behind me now.

I had crossed the line.

29

There was another direction open to me. It was a direction that I had not moved in before, but which felt completely familiar. I moved towards it, somehow, and I was ripped out of time.

No, I was ripped out of space. It was time that I was in. It is time that we are always in.

I felt like a mouse that had spent his entire life following a road, only to be picked up by a hawk and dragged up into the sky. From there I could finally see the whole road at once - the entire road, and everything that connected to it and everything that related to it. I could now see the path of the road, how it hugged rivers, followed valleys, avoided mountains and forests, and I could finally understand where it was going. From my viewpoint I could now see both where it started, and where it ended. What made little sense from a mouse-eye perspective was now clear, even obvious.

I saw that all events on that road existed regardless of whether I had already passed through them, or whether I had yet to experience them. They were like the roads we had driven on and the towns we had passed through on our journey round the coast. We were at the bottom of Cornwall, yet everywhere we had travelled still existed, from Portmeirion to the Hill

O'Many Stanes, from Blackpool to Brighton. So did every road in between, every yard, every inch. Time was no different. It was all there, eternal. Every last second.

My life was laid out in front of me in exquisite detail, and I plunged back into it.

30

It is mid-afternoon and her bedroom window is open. The breeze lifts her curtains and stops the warm air inside from stagnating. It carries the scents from the herb garden and the nearby meadows, scents of late May or early June. They are subtle and gently intermingle with her perfume.

We aren't doing anything but resting. We lie entwined on the bed, comfortable enough with both the silence and the position. Penny had often said that our bodies fitted together perfectly, whatever their positions. We are young.

There is no pressure to talk, or kiss, or plan. The breeze brushes over my skin, and the music from the tape deck is sweet and honest and everywhere.

There is no great revelation at this time; all is natural and carefree and all is right with the moment. The future casts no shadows. But I am starting to understand something. I had previously thought that love was an insane thing, the impulse behind obsessions and uncontrollable infatuations. It was sweet madness, I had thought, dangerous and volatile and blind, and no good could come from it. What can I say, I was a teenager and an idiot, and that was the sort of thing I used to think back then. I thought that attitude was impressive.

But the love I feel this afternoon has shown this for folly. I see those lesser feelings and emotions for what they are. They are side effects and shadows and symptoms, but in themselves they are little and of no consequence. The love at their source has no baggage, it contains no jealousies or cruelty or problems. It is pure and untainted, and it fills the room during these moments. Love is the silence that drowns out all the noise.

There is much that is sublime, but only one moment can be the pinnacle of a life, the pivot around which all else revolves. I am in that moment. I see that it is eternal, and that it can never fade.

Love comes in waves, and there must always be a high tide.

So I spend a thousand lifetimes here.

31

I am in a pub on Charing Cross Road in London. Johnny is holding court - you know Johnny, everyone knows Johnny. When is this? Five years ago? Ten maybe? I take a long swig of my beer. The pub is warm. I am happy.

Johnny has long sideburns that consider meeting under his chin and a permanent half-smile that lives more in his eyes than on his chin. He has taken to wearing a plaster on his left temple – we'd all be doing it this time next year – and is seemingly addressing his thoughts to the corner of the roof.

'I reckon I know what heaven's like', he says. 'It's where they sit you down and show you a videotape of your whole life, except that they've edited out all the bad bits and the boring stuff, and just left all your best bits. Your best rounds of pool, the best goals you've ever scored. Your best jokes and your best sex, the times it goes right and you just rock. And you can sit there and think, 'Yeah! That's me!' And you've got a remote control and a drink and a really comfy chair and you've got as long as you like to watch it.'

And everyone laughs and nods, and the evening slips along.

I am four and watching cartoons at my grandparents' house. The phone is ringing in the hallway. I watch my father walk out of the room towards it, then turn back to Bugs Bunny.

And there is a horrible cry, short and sharp and painful, and people are rushing out of the room towards my father. 'Victoria's dead,' they are saying, 'Victoria's dead.' Which is funny, because Victoria is my mother's name.

And then my father is back in the room, and I had never seen my father crying before, and I throw both of my arms around his legs and hold them tight, and I am crying himself.

My father's hand rests on my head and I look up as he looks down at me, with a smile of great kindness despite his tears. 'Don't cry Russ, he says, 'You don't need to cry. It's me who needs to cry.'

I am at the dentist, gently reclined, mouth agape. The hygienist's polishing tool is shaking tooth after tooth. My gums are bleeding and she keeps working, scraping between tooth and gum, cleaning bone and hurting nerve. My hands grip the arm rests tight, my nails sink into the black leather. The pain is bearable, just, but not if it doesn't end soon.

Unhurried, the hygienist moves the rotating polishing tool to another tooth, agitating another sensitive set of nerves. How long has this been going on for now? Surely she must finish soon? But she doesn't. She slowly and methodically continued with her work. Seconds grow into minutes, and the sharp, smothering pain remains steady. I feel all that again.

I am meeting Will for the first time. He pokes his head into our old rehearsal room, unsure if he is in the right place. Me and Pen are trying to look nonchalant, casually tuning up and acting as inscrutable as possible. We are hiding the fact that we are a couple, because that's what you do if you're in a band and a couple. Will stumbles over a few words, checking that we were ready for his audition. I nod and he slinks back out of the room and goes to unload his kit from the car. I ask Penny what she thinks.

'Terrible first impression,' she says. 'He'll be the one, though.'

I wonder how she knows these things.

'Would you mind?' Penny asks me. It is coming up to Christmas, and we have some time off from the band. She is considering going up and spending some time with her family. Would I mind? No, I wouldn't mind.

So much has happened to us in the first couple of years of the band. We have barely stopped moving. We have not had time to accept how different we are now, or how much we have learnt and changed. We understand ourselves as a couple, but we no longer know who we are as individuals. We would need to be apart to understand that, to look at who we are now and compare ourselves with who we were.

I pull the appropriate faces and say the appropriate words. I know the couple script and I can recite it automatically. If that is what you want then of course I understand and yes of course you should go. Of course I'll miss you but don't worry about me. I'll be fine.

Later that evening, I will reflect on how it was Penny that asked for the time apart, and not myself.

I am watching TV. Hours of TV, on different sets in different houses. My numbed mind stares at the disconnected images, hypnotised and asleep. Christ, it was bad enough the first time round, but to see it all again is deadening. My heart slowly pumps the blood around my passive body, but the body almost does not need it. My living self has regressed from animal down to somewhere near vegetable. There are occasions, it's true, where the TV causes emotions to spark in my mind, and fear or wonder or laughter registers. But they are shallow echoes of genuine emotions. They are tricked into materialising only to find that there is nothing to interact with. Their cause has already departed, oblivious to what it had triggered. The wasted emotions dwindle down alone, never reaching their potential.

I flick past programme after programme. It was bad enough first time, but now I already know what is going to happen. Everything is a repeat.

There are years of this shit.

That guy from the record company puts the phone down. I stare at him. He nods. I grin.

I have been asked to record the lead song for the soundtrack of a big, star-studded rom-com. This is, touch wood, a guarantee of a hit single. The song is a big, overwrought ballad that does not skimp on sentimentality.

'We've got to think about this very carefully,' he says. 'This is an opportunity, but it is also a curse. The song is shit. But it will be a hit. You will have a career. It will be the career of a singer known for a shit song. We must think very carefully before agreeing.

'I quite like it,' I told him.

'That's irrelevant. You like everything. You must think about what will happen if you do become known for this.'

'You need to think about what my career will be like if I don't do this,' I said.

He thought about this. He picked up the phone.

'I'll tell them you're eager to get going and have some notes on the demo, he said as he dialled.

I glanced left, and I glanced right. Johnny was nearly right, but it was not a highlights tape. I glanced up and I glanced down. I glanced through and I glanced behind. It was all there. All of it. Every boring bus journey. Every night time hour slept away. Every word, every action, every thought. Every cruel comment, every laugh, every piss.

It was marvellous.

I dived back in.

It was the physical stuff that worked best. The sex and dancing, running and performing, eating and shitting. Why was that, why was that so rewarding to revisit now? Perhaps it was rarity - there just wasn't enough of it. Not the amount of shitting, of course. I got that about right. But the total amount of sex and dancing and running and performing came as a bit of a shock. Would it have killed me to have spent less time on the Nintendo?

Sex. She was sweet and drunk and she looked familiar, but it wasn't Penny. What was her name? Her arms and legs were flung out, bending at 90 degree angles at the knees and elbows. Her form was symmetrical and geometric, like a carving from some forgotten pre-Roman city. Wow, where did that image come from? That was elaborate, wasn't it? But of course - I am drunk. My head is full of wine. I am revelling.

It was slow and relaxed, and tinged with a flavour of something that I could feel but not yet place. What was it? I was not lying on her, but supported myself on my knees and my outstretched arms, keeping my distance, enjoying moving freely towards and away. This is too much information, isn't it? You don't need to know this. But it is important in some way. Something is about to happen. I have to keep going with this.

I am feeling her emotions washing through her. I am feeling what she is feeling. There is my touch, there are my sensations. They were separate from my own but neither eclipse the other. How had I not noticed this before? It was empathy. I was aware of every reaction to my actions.

Wait a second - it was always like this. That empathy was always present. I'd never noticed. I'd just never noticed. How could I have missed that?

I moved forward, absorbed in both the action and the reaction. Yet that wasn't it, the strange flavour that I mentioned earlier. Something was forbidden about this, I realised, and I was enjoying that. I withdrew, unhurried, until I could go no farther back without slipping out. Who had opened the door?

It was Penny. She stood frozen in the bedroom doorway. I froze too. The girl below me froze as well.

An age passed.

Eyes glanced between eyes. Expressions were fixed. No-one spoke. No-one blinked.

Shame, embarrassment, betrayal, they all filled the room, a horrible wave that came from all three of us. It was damage somehow, clamped, compressed, wrong, terrible.

Christ, how long would this last for? Oh, it's going to get worse. Oh, the low point is coming. The worst moment. There must always be a worst moment but, please, not this.

My arms were starting to hurt. My elbows were at an odd angle. I couldn't keep supporting himself in that position much longer.

No, I was going to have to move. But move how? I lowered himself down slowly. I slid back into her, I didn't mean to but I did. Ah, it felt so sweet. Below, I was aware of the shivers that ran through the woman's body. How she loved that!

Tell me this didn't happen.

It was wrong. My gut shouted that this was wrong. I moved away from her, pulling out. My heart was pounding and my brain was away, so there was little that could hide the sweetness. Slowly I turned my gaze back to Penny. Her face was still unchanged, her body unmoving. That position was no better, my arms still felt weak, I couldn't keep my weight balanced so. Keeping my gaze on Penny, I slid back in.

I did. Forgive me, that is what happened.

Penny's leg gave. She caught herself before she collapsed, and she turned and stumbled and left the house. And then I felt it. I felt Penny's heart break. It was blunt and sudden, and its awful dull echoes will never leave me.

I looked at the empty doorframe. I started to cry. I cried because I hurt. I hurt because I had wounded.

32

Now that I had become conscious of the feelings of others, I could no longer avoid them. Wherever I was in my life, there they were.

They were only acknowledged subconsciously at the time, but that empathy layer was always there. Every action had its response. Every emotion I caused was clear and strong, regardless of whether they occurred in me or in others. I felt the gratitude caused by kind words and thoughtful acts. These were little things I had done automatically and forgotten the moment they happened, unaware of the value others placed on them. And then there were the cruel acts, spiteful and ugly, and I felt the anger and the hurt that those caused.

But there were also the times where I caused hurt without meaning to, without even noticing. The important conversations brushed aside when my mind was elsewhere, the forgotten birthdays, the tactless comments.

There was no malice in any of them. My thoughts were simply elsewhere, but that did not prevent the reactions from hurting. And my mind was so often elsewhere, amusing itself, playing out unreal scenarios of no value or consequence, more focused on its own fancies than the reality that never stopped around it. So there was a lot of this. An awful lot.

These were different to the times when I focused so hard that I lost the world around me. Times spent songwriting, playing, learning new instruments. Times spent observing, studying the world in macro, noticing the play of light on form - all that felt positive and worthwhile. The problem was when I had been favouring an internal world over the world around me. And this was by far the majority of my preoccupied moments.

I became aware of a sense of judgement resulting from my words and actions. There was an approval or disapproval rating attached to everything. I could not complain about this, for I knew that the judge was myself.

Initially this judgement was in my gut, but once it had been recognised it made sense to formalise it. So I assigned it a numerical value and projected it on the screen of my mind's eye as a score. I experimented with a few different fonts until I found one that I was happy with.

So the score went up when I caused positive reactions and it went down to mark the opposite. The scoring system was arcane and unknowable, complete with bonuses, bonus multipliers and harsh penalties, but it never felt unfair or wrong. The digits whirled and rotated and reacted to every moment in every second across the whole of my life.

When I was onstage, in front of a large crowd, and the gig was going well, those figures would be a blur. When the entire crowd was feeling good because of what I was doing, those numbers would be through the roof.

But that wasn't often. More frequently, I was draining it.

There were long periods when it would turn negative.

33

I answer the door to an old man with a white beard and silver hair. He is short, about 5'3". 'Hello Russell,' he says, 'I'm Orlando Monk!'

'Fuck off!' I say automatically. He laughs and walks past me, into my home.

I follow him into the kitchen in a daze. I try to remember if I have mentioned that name to anyone. How can there be someone claiming that name? I jotted it down in a notebook months ago, but no-one has seen it.

I am aware that I am in a state of shock. I am also aware that he knows this, and is amused by it. If I had known that at the time it would have angered me, but from my current perspective I can see his point.

'You're going to be a little bit shocked to see me, but that's your own fault. If you invent a fictitious character with the power to leave the world of fiction and come into the material world, then you're going to have to put up with this sort of stuff.'

I look at him. He is making tea.

'You are much older than Orlando Monk,' I tell him. He shrugs.

'I am very, very old, you are right. That doesn't make it polite to mention it.'

'Orlando Monk isn't old,' I say.

'No-one's old at first, you idiot. You did insist on making me a time traveller. That means we have to put up with these disconnects.'

'I knew that was a bad idea!'

Orlando shrugs, but I think he agrees with me.

'But listen,' I say, 'I haven't written anything about Orlando Monk. I've decided not to be a writer. So it's a bit presumptuous of you to arrive in my kitchen and start making tea.'

'Oh, fuck off. I'll arrive in any kitchen I damn well please. Do you know how frustrating it is to be a fictitious character which your creator can't be arsed to use? Have you any idea what that is like? Milk or sugar?' he asks.

'Just milk.'

He puts the milk in the mugs. The kettle boils.

'I declared myself public domain.'

'You did what?'

'I put myself in the public domain.'

'You can't do that!'

'Tough. You abandoned me, so I did it. Anyway, that's not why I'm here. I'm here on a kindness. I've just seen you by the red van. That won't mean anything to you now, so don't worry about that. But you seemed lost and I thought I owed you something. I've come to give you a bit of advice.'

'I don't care if you've come to mend the boiler. I want to know how this is possible.'

He hands me the mug of tea.

'Your current thinking is showing signs of the confusion that I want to talk to you about. You think that you can decide whether to write a book, or decide to not write a book? You think that you're in charge of your actions and that you can choose to create the non-real things in your head? I'm not criticising. That's just normal. It's total bullshit of course, but that's hardly your fault. Come on, sit down.'

We both sit at the kitchen table.

'If you focus only on the real world then eventually you're going to notice that nothing makes any sense, and that's going to upset you, and you're going to have a bad time. When you look around and see the material world is how it is because the immaterial has made it that way, then things will not be so bleak. The material is important, no doubt about that, and the interplay between real and not-real is very complicated. But I'm speaking as someone who is both real and imaginary, so you can listen to me on this. Ultimately, the material is the immaterial's bitch.'

'Russell, things happen. You can either accept them or fight against them. Think of it this way: There's a river. It's high and fast-flowing, and it twists and turns on its way to the sea. Now, imagine that a stick falls into it, and that stick is flowing downriver. What if that stick was to think, 'I don't like being here. I should be nearer the centre of the river, or nearer the bank or whatever. Then the stick puts all its efforts into getting to that position. But what can it do? It can't do anything, it's a stick. But what does the river do? Well it may leave the stick where it is, or even move it in the wrong direction. In which case, the stick will get upset and angry. It won't understand why it isn't going where it wants. It will get bitter, and think that everything is unfair and unjust. The stick has achieved nothing, in other words, but its own unhappiness. What though, if the river moved the stick where it wanted to go? The stick will think that it did that! The stick will get an unreal understanding of its own power. It will become arrogant. It will be a smug stick.'

'But think about this: Imagine the stick does not try to go either left or right. Instead it understands that it is a stick in a river, and the river is taking it somewhere, and that it can't really do anything about that. But it knows that it won't come to any harm, because it's a stick in a river. If that happens, then it will notice that being a stick being washed downriver is a lot of fun. It's like water slides, but without the chlorine. Do you get my point?'

We are silent, sizing each other up.

'A stick can't think,' I say. 'It's just a stick.'

He leans across and slaps me hard across my face. He points his index finger at me.

'Always allow the artist his metaphor,' he says. 'If you learn one thing in life, one thing to stop you being an ignorant fuckhead and a total buzzkill, then make it that.'

34

I am sitting in the pub in Blackpool. It is mid-afternoon and the light streams sideways into the dark bar. I am listening to Penny's music. I have drunk half a pint of Guinness. I have crisps.

My eyes are closed. I am aware of Penny arriving and sitting next to me. I am aware of her hand resting on top of mine.

I am listening.

Music is alien. It is not a resident of our material world. It comes from elsewhere. It doesn't exist in space. It exists in time. Sure, there are instruments, and musicians, and they vibrate air, and they create sound. But it is not music unless it is heard. Sound needs memory to become music. Rhythm and melody must play out in time.

How strange that some things don't need to exist in space, yet they still exist.

Music is a path. We join it at the start and we follow it.

We were listening intently, Penny and I. We listened so deeply, back then, that it was all we were aware of. I was not aware of my Guinness. I was not aware of my crisps. We had slipped out of the physical world and we hung in the temporal.

Except there was her hand on mine, and I was aware of that hand. It was an anchor. It kept me in the physical world of space and the temporal world of music simultaneously. And because those moments exist forever, I can reach back to them from here. That music was a path and that path was a bridge.

I was on that bridge. It was the awareness of her hand that kept the bridge solid. Solid enough to pass over.

I could feel something nearby. Over my shoulder, perhaps, or behind me. Something that was waiting for me. Ah, was it really time to go already?

How had I done? I glanced at the score. The numbers were still rolling too fast to read, scores being added and removed a trillion times a second. I hurried it up.

The final tally appeared. It said, 'Score: 0000000067'.

'Level completed. Congratulations.'

I thought about this. Could have been worse.

Then came the words, 'Previous Hi-Score: 0083626143.' I suspect that was a joke.

'Loading...'

It was time to go. Over my shoulder I felt the summoning. I looked across at Penny as she listened to her music, breathing slowly with eyes closed, a resting face free from cares and concerns, a half smile of exquisite purity. And I turned, and returned.

35

I am wrenched upwards. I gasp for breath and I hear myself gasp. My arms flay around, operating automatically. There is a hand. It doesn't rest gently on mine. It grips, too tight, and it bruises. It pulls at my upper arm.

Here is Will. It is Will's hand. He is dragging me out of the water.

I am slumped on the rocks. They are cold and hard and slimy. I am coughing, or trying to. I am wrenching water out of my lungs. I throw the sea water up, and it spreads over the rocks and disappears into the slime.

'Fucking hell Russ!', says Will.

Soon I am up on my knees. He is leading me away from the water's edge. He is jabbering away. He seems shocked, and annoyed, and excited. I gather that I hit the water close to where he was and scared the life out of him. Also, the splash from my fall soaked him. This seems to be a particular sticking point. He is babbling away but keeps returning to his soaking.

'How long was I under?', I ask.

'Long enough to get a lungful,' he tells me. 'Five seconds maybe. Ten at most.'

Ten seconds?

I am shivering. He leads me back up the path. He is worried that if I don't get some dry clothes on soon I will catch pneumonia. He is clutching his plastic sample case, and the bottles inside rattle as we walk. The path is steep.

Penny is standing at the top of the path, holding her spade. She sees us coming towards her. Will sees her also.

'Penny!' he shouts, and waves up at her. 'He fell in the sea!'

'I know!' she calls back.

'He nearly drowned! I fished him out just in time.'

'Fat lot of help you are!'

Will doesn't catch her meaning. She walks down towards us. I stop, and stumble. She raises the spade as she approaches. She is going for another swing.

I watch to see how this plays out.

She looks more agitated this time. Less certain. More annoyed. She looks me in the eye and holds my gaze.

She brings the spade through the air, towards my face, and she lets out a cry.

This will really hurt, I think to myself. I brace for impact.

Will's plastic case appears in front of me.

I look at him. He stands between me and Penny, with a horrified look on his face. He has just understood what is happening. He brings the case upwards, shielding me, stopping the blow.

The case crumples under the blow. I hear glass bottles inside shatter.

Things go fast now. Penny grunts, and tries another attack. Will steps in front of her, holding the remains of his case with both hands. He uses it to shield himself from the blow. The spade's shaft cracks. The case splits open. Blue bottles spill out on the floor.

Penny looks disbelievingly at the broken spade handle in her hand. Will looks at the broken bottles bouncing on the path, rolling down towards the sea. I look at Penny. She looks like a scared child.

Slowly, I stand and walk towards her. I put my arms around her, and tell her that it is all right. For a moment her body is rigid, but then it slumps.

She drops the spade handle, and starts to cry.

I tell her that everything is well, and that she has done all that she needs to, and that I am sorry for everything. She doesn't reply, but she lets me hold her.

Will is perplexed. I can feel him watching us, trying to understand. He is trying to work out if he or I are in danger. Then he understands that the moment has tipped, and frantically dashes down the path in search of his escaping bottles.

36

Dawn found us sitting by the van with the campfire still burning. Will was methodically assessing his collection. The case had undergone a successful repair, of sorts, with gaffer tape and with some good old-fashioned bashing into shape. The bottles, both those broken and those still intact, had been gathered together and now lay in a watery mess inside the case. All the pages had been gathered together, and Will was methodically checking every one and putting them in order.

He then checked them again, to make certain that none were missing. Satisfied, he smiled up at me and Penny.

'That's the lot', he said. 'That's the complete text.'

'Give us a reading, then,' asked Penny.

'Do I have to?' he said. 'You can have a read of them yourself if you like.'

'Read!'

'You're getting me all self-conscious now. They'll sound stupid read out.'

'Tough. You collected them, you have to read them out.'

Will stood and awkwardly shuffled through the papers.

'Tell you what,' he said, 'I'll give you one from the spoiler section at the back. They're short.'

'They have a spoiler section?' I asked.

'Oh man, they have all sorts. Are you ready?'

Me and Pen nodded. He began to read.

'From the spoiler section of the saner bible. Here we go: In the beginning was the Word. And that Word was 'again'. In the end was also the Word. This annoys the pedants, who insist that the end should be a full stop. Get annoyed all you like, pedants! The end will still be the Word. You won't know what that Word is, however, until it passes your lips.'

We gave him a polite round of applause.

He put the pages carefully into the inside pocket of his coat and tapped out a celebratory drum roll on the plastic case with his fingers.

We sat in silence for some time, and watched the sun rise. Light and heat, man. Light and heat.

My face was sore, and swollen. I did not mind.

Will leaned forward and started beating out a slow 4/4 rhythm on his plastic case. ONE two three four, ONE two three four, ONE two three four, ONE two three four.

After a while Penny began humming a melody over the top. It was hesitant at first, and far more sparse than anything I had heard her come up with before. It had the air of a lament. Will kept the rhythm going with his left hand as he reached out to collect a stick from near the fire. He used this stick on the side of the case to build a more intricate pattern, echoing back some cues from Penny.

I listened for a while and then joined in at a lower register, alternating between adding a bass part to Will's drumming and harmonising with Penny. We kept this up for eight bars, then sixteen, then as one we changed it into something new. We were all improvising, of course, yet we were improvising as one. None of our parts made sense by themselves. Together, however, they understood each other perfectly. We kept going by instinct, being too surprised by the overall sound to think too deeply about our individual contribution. The lament had become brighter, and celebratory. It was a delight.

We think that this world is ours, don't we? We think that it's the planet of people, and that people do stuff like making music. This world isn't ours. Music was here a long time before we arrived. It was here before we recorded, or wrote it down as a score, or danced to the drums around the communal fire. The birds sang before we did, and the whales before them. It will continue long after you or I have gone. It will continue after mankind has gone. Those cockroaches will make some amazing sounds. We are temporary. Music is not.

You cannot turn it off. You can only listen, or dance.

Together, Will, Penny and I made our music.

37

The van slipped through the traffic like a snake through grass. In slow graceful arcs it overtook and undertook, and junctions, bends and roundabouts eased obediently out of its way. Speed cameras watched spellbound, forgetting to capture the van on film, for they were not used to seeing such grace on the A27, especially from such an old, filthy Ford Transit.

We turned off the A27 at Chichester and onto the road that started it all, the A259. We journeyed in silence through Bognor Regis, Littlehampton and Worthing, because where there was understanding there was no need for conversation. The sun was low in the sky behind us as we passed the gas works at Portslade and drove towards Brighton along the elegant Hove seafront. The road had indeed taken us along the edge of an island. The journey was circular, but the place we will arrive at will not be the place we left. We started from the coast of Britain and returned to the coast of Albion.

When the West Pier appeared in view Will pulled over and parked. This was not a journey that we were going to finish that day. We were not ready to return to society and besides, there was something we still had to do. Society could wait one more night for us.

I only realised that it wasn't the Palace Pier, the start of our journey, when I stepped out of the van and noticed that the front section of the structure had slumped into the sea. A larger, Victorian ballroom stood in the water behind it, and the walkway that had linked it to the collapsed front section pointed down at 45 degrees, plunging into the surf. This was the abandoned West Pier; the lights and bustle of the Palace Pier lay a few hundred yards further down the road. My memory of this pier was that it was considerably more ruined than this, that it was nothing but a shell of twisted iron stranded out to sea. But then memory is a strange thing.

Flocks of starlings, many thousand in number, circled and danced around the ballroom, as if to celebrate its freedom and release from the land. The setting sun lit the rotten timbers and rusting ironwork in a warm orange glow and gave the building a sense of power and dignity that it must have lacked in its glory days. Its age gave it a look of peace and wisdom.

It was perfect.

We gathered what we would need for the night in three bin bags, inflated them with air, and sealed them as best we could with knots and tape. Taking a bag each we strolled into the sea, feeling the cold but unconcerned by it, and we swam out to the ballroom. The waves churned and eddied through the iron legs of the pier, tossing us swimmers about, but we managed to grab onto the ironwork and climb up onto the wooden deck. Ignoring the 'Warning! Unsafe Structure' signs we forced a rotten door and entered the Ballroom. We passed through the lobby.

The low sun glowed through the shattered windows along the western side of the cavernous hall. It gave the huge space the appearance and feel of a long forgotten cathedral. The sky was darker out of the East windows. A long progression of white lights could be seen along the length of the Palace Pier, travelling away from the land and out into the sea like a progression of pilgrims marching away from the land they knew into an abyss they did not.

Inside it smelt of salt and bird crap and rot. The cries of the starlings competed with the cries of the sea, and the air felt alive and potent.

In the centre of the hall, we unpacked the camping equipment.

Penny stretched a T-shirt over the cooking pot while Will opened his green plastic carry case. The water sloshed around the bottom, and the shards of blue broken glass glittered among it. He poured the water slowly through the T-Shirt, sieving out the glass, sea weed and larger bits of crud. Penny put the pan on the camping stove and turned up the flame. The pan had no lid so he placed the teapot over it, helping it to boil quicker and warming the teapot at the same time.

'We're going to have to decide if we're going around again', said Will. It was the first thing that anyone had said for many hours. Penny and I nodded. She pulled the mugs and teabags out of her bag.

The seawater started to bubble. West coast sea mingled with east coast, Scottish water merged with Welsh. The island's moat moved and swam amongst itself, each part containing the essence of all its constituents, the whole becoming more than the sum of its parts. The water boiled.

I sniffed the milk, noted that it was off, and poured it in the mugs anyway. Penny added a couple of tea bags into the pot and poured the boiling water over them. She held the pot by the handle and spout and swirled it round three times. The water flowed through the bags and emerged the colour of earth.

Will started to giggle as the tea was poured out. Penny and I looked at him and understood, and we too grinned wide crazy grins.

'Cheers!' said Will, and we clinked our mugs. Then we sat in silence, and we drank the tea.

stop here

ITINERARY

DAY ONE: Brighton, East Sussex – Sandwich Bay, Kent

DAY TW0: Sandwich Bay – Clacton-on-Sea

DAY THREE: Clacton-on-Sea – Kings Lynn

DAY FOUR: Kings Lynn – Whitby

DAY FIVE: Whitby – Berwick Upon Tweed

DAY SIX: Berwick Upon Tweed – St. Andrews

DAY SEVEN: St. Andrews – Aberdeen

DAY EIGHT: Aberdeen – Nairn

DAY NINE: Nairn – Hill O'Many Staines

DAY TEN: Hill O'Many Staines – Tongue

DAY ELEVEN: Tongue – Inverewe Gardens

DAY TWELVE: Inverewe Gardens – Salen

DAY THIRTEEN: Salen – Oban

DAY FOURTEEN: Oban – Glasgow

DAY FIFTEEN: Glasgow – Stranraer

DAY SIXTEEN: Stranraer – Carlisle

DAY SEVENTEEN: Carlisle – Liverpool

DAY EIGHTEEN: Liverpool – Caernarfon

DAY NINETEEN: Caernarfon – St David's Head

DAY TWENTY: St David's Head – Cardiff

DAY TWENTY ONE: Cardiff – Weston-Super-Mare

DAY TWENTY TWO: Weston-Super-Mare – Bude

DAY TWENTY THREE: Bude – Hell's Mouth

DAY TWENTY FOUR: Hell's Mouth – Lizard

DAY TWENTY FIVE: Lizard – Plymouth

DAY TWENTY SIX: Plymouth – Portland Bill

DAY TWENTY SEVEN: Portland Bill – Selsey Bill

DAY TWENTY EIGHT: Selsey Bill – Brighton

BY THE SAME AUTHOR:

KLF: CHAOS MAGIC MUSIC MONEY

They were the best-selling singles band in the world. They had awards, credibility, commercial success and creative freedom.

They then deleted their records, erased themselves from musical history and burnt their last million pounds in a boathouse on the Isle of Jura.

But they couldn't say why.

This is the story of The KLF, told through the ideas that drove them. It is a story about Carl Jung, Alan Moore, Robert Anton Wilson, Ken Campbell, Dada, Situationism, Discordianism, magic, chaos, punk, rave and the alchemical symbolism of Doctor Who.

Wildly unauthorised and unlike any other music biography, this is a trawl through chaos on a hunt for meaning.

(P) THE BIG HAND 2012
ISBN 978-0-9564163-8-4
Available on Kindle and paperback.

I HAVE AMERICA SURROUNDED: THE LIFE OF
TIMOTHY LEARY

The brilliant first biography of the man President Nixon
called 'the most dangerous man in America'.

Timothy Leary was one of the most controversial and
divisive figures of the twentieth century. President Nixon called
him 'the most dangerous man in America.' Hunter S.
Thompson said that he was 'not just wrong, but a treacherous
creep and a horrible goddamn person.' Yet the writer Terence
McKenna claims that he 'probably made more people happy
than anyone else in history.'

A brilliant Harvard psychologist, Leary was sacked because
of his research into LSD and other psychedelic drugs. He went
on to become the global figurehead of the 1960s drug culture,
coin the phrase 'tune in, turn on and drop out', and persuade
millions of people to take drugs and explore alternative
lifestyles yet the tremendous impact of his 'scandalous' research
has been so controversial that it has completely overshadowed
the man himself and the details of his life. Few people realise
that Timothy Leary's life is one of the greatest untold adventure
stories of the twentieth century.

Timothy Leary led a life of unflagging optimism and
reckless devotion to freedom. It was, in the words of his
goddaughter Winona Ryder, 'not just epic grandeur but flat-
out epic grandeur.' Leary's life is undoubtedly one of the

greatest untold adventure stories of the twentieth century and this book presents it for the first time in all its uncensored glory.

(P) THE FRIDAY PROJECT 2006
ISBN 978-1905548255
Available on Kindle and paperback.

Orlando Monk will return

in

The First Church on the Moon

Lightning Source UK Ltd.
Milton Keynes UK
UKOW04f2303050813

214918UK00005B/751/P

9 780956 416353